Duffle Bag Bitches

By

Alicia Howard

Duffle Bag Bitches

© Revised 2016 by Alicia C. Howard

Alicia Howard Present

Saint Louis, Mo

Prologue

Dallas sat there on a bench in the Wellston Loop thinking about Kesha and how he let the love of his life slip through his fucking hands. She is gone now and there is nothing he could do about it. Sometimes in this life you're bound to lose the one you hold near and dear to your heart.

That's part doesn't bother him, but the fact that he has never told her how he really felt about her. He doesn't know shit about square love. All he knows is hustling and pimping. It's in his blood his mother Sadie was a whore and his father was her pimp. Hustling is something he picked up along the way. Niggas likes to floss too hard he wants to show them how to shining is stupid.

Dallas is a thoroughbred ass nigga. He doesn't take any shit from anyone. That isn't in his blood he is a nigga that feels that its either kill or be killed. He isn't ever gonna bitch up no matter how real or ill shit gets around him.

He vows to never see the inside of a jail. When his time comes he would hold court in the streets. He is originally from Portland, Oregon, relocated to St. Louis,

Missouri on the run from the feds for dope charges.

Dallas is a sexy chocolate nigga. He stands five eleven, one hundred sixty-five pounds, and rocking a deep wave fade with a goatee. He has a set of teeth so pearly white that he could do a commercial for Crest.

The swag he has is insane! He has bitches selling pussy out of love and not out of fear. But lately his mind has been playing tricks on him. Dallas has been thinking about Kesha a lot. She would be in his dreams asking him why he didn't save her.

Every time he tries to explain it she would fade away. *He would wake up looking for her. The truth of the matter was she was dead and a small piece of him had died with her. He often blames himself for her death because she put him on to the lick.*

He knows she should have never been setting niggas up to be robbed in the first place. Dallas thought women were soft, sensual creatures that a man was supposed to love and protect. That's exactly what he provided for the women that worked for him.

Dallas never hit them or forced them to work the strip; it was something that they were already doing when they met him. He offered them safety, love, and money management skills. That's why Kesha didn't mind working for him before she got down with her own crew STL Finest.

The last lick they did together came back to bite them in the ass in the end. Kesha had gotten her head blown off by a 12-gauge shot gun. There is no coming back from that. It's funny how fast shit change right before your eyes. That happened two years ago

Today Dallas is the man. His squad, the Duffle Bag Crew run shit. Dallas has always been able to sweet talk bitches into doing anything he said. That's how he made a living over the years. He stepped his game up from just pimping hoes to busting niggas down to size.

Shit is running smoothly but sometimes you just can't send a man to do a woman's job. Niggas loves women so he felt by adding some to his crew. He could easily bring in more money that's. That is how the Duffle Bag bitches were born.

Dallas set out to find a different breed of bitch. Not the kind that laid down *and spread them wide to eat. The kind*

that blows your fucking head off taking

what the fuck she needs to survive. He

has trained them extremely well.

They know he is the master. If he

hadn't done that, he knows that one of

them bitches might have bit him taking

over his whole operation.

Shannon, Jasmine, Nisha, and Jay

are his thoroughbreds. He never fucked

any of them, not because he doesn't want

to, but because he couldn't. The Duffle Bag

Bitches name rings in the streets so hard

muthafuckas know three things about

them: They work for Dallas Palmer; they

are the baddest bitches you will ever meet. They don't give a fuck about nothing but Dallas and money.

They have hit every hustler that shined too hard from St. Louis to L.A. If you had it, then D. Palmer wants it. There is nothing stopping these hoes from getting it and bringing it back to Daddy. Even though they never gave him any pussy. They love him for who he us and what he has done for them.

CHAPTER 1

Two Years Earlier

Nisha is 5'7," one hundred and fifteen pounds, and the color of caramel on an ice cream sundae. She wears jet black Remy weave that hung to the middle of her back. She met Dallas a few years back when she was dating this nigga named West.

She had been shacking up with him for a year and a half made the nigga think she was head over heels in love with him, but she wasn't.

Nisha watched West do his thing for a while before she stepped to him. She needed to see what type of bitches he likes. Once she realizes she fit the shoes, she got on his ass. Nisha fucked and sucked him the first night she met him.

She blew the niggas mind. After just one hit of the pussy he was hooked. He was a good dude he did her right, but she wasn't looking for love. Nisha and her crew were only looking for a come-up.

Dallas' crew kidnapped Nisha ass to get West to pay the ransom. Nisha didn't know if he would. Since Dallas and his crew didn't harm her in any way. She let Dallas in on why she was fucking with

West for real, and how he was fucking with her money.

Dallas had to laugh at that little frail ass bitch. She has the heart of a lion times ten. West paid the ransom of one hundred and fifty G's for her, but it didn't move or change her plans. It just bought him six more months to live.

Dallas told Nisha that if her crew made it back to him alive after taking West out. Then he would put them on to some major players in several different states.

It was the Fourth of July when Nisha set shit off with West. They were fucking strong, but that is the only thing she loved about him. *"Oooh daddy hit that shit!"* Nisha moans. When she talks like that it drives West wild.

"Bitch whose pussy is this?" West asks. Nisha didn't say shit because she has a complex with the bitch word. It's what caused her to kill her stepfather. West used it a lil' too much for her liking.

"Bitch whose pussy is this?" he barks again.

Nisha plays her part, *"Yours daddy! Ooohhh Aaahhh daddy it's yours!"* she yelled. West was so into it that he never heard the door open. He tilts his head back as he busts a load off in her. He was always trying to get her pregnant, but the bitch bought the morning after pills by the case. She takes one after every fuck session.

As West came he also went home to meet his maker. The bullet from a silenced .357 shatters his brain. Jasmine made her way into the house. Through the back door Nisha left open for her. She crept into the room standing there watching them fuck for two reasons.

One she is a certified freak and the other is because she loves catching niggas with their pants down.

Jasmine is five-foot-four, one hundred and thirty-five pounds with golden brown skin. She wears her hair in strawberry red curls that made her look like an exotic Pocahontas. She slumped West so fast he thought it was the nut he busted putting him to sleep.

Nisha kicks West off the back of the bed causing his neck to break when he lands. First a bullet to the back of the head, then a broken neck. Ain't no coming back from that. "Damn bitch you were moving in slow motion. I know your freaky ass was watching the show," Nisha yells.

Jasmine dying laughing. "Bitch your skinny ass sure knows how to throw that pussy." She holds her stomach cracking up like there isn't a dead man a foot away from her.

"Bitch let's get this money so we can get out of here and meet up with Dallas." Nisha has a crush on him, but it doesn't matter because she never gonna fuck him. She needs to know that he respects her G code.

They gathered up the four hundred thousand dollars that he was saving to buy Nisha that million-dollar house she always said she wanted. He was in love with her for real. Sadly, she was too blind and hurt from life to see it.

Nisha and Jasmine hops in the white Chevy idling outside with Shannon and Big Jay casing the scene. Making sure no one came to the house before they finished the job. The four girls peeled off. Shannon is driving like a damn fool as always.

"Slow this muthafucka down hoe!" Big Jay yells at her.

"Bitch I got this, with yo' dirty ass." Shannon is forever calling a muthafucka dirty. She thinks she is the shit. Shannon is 5'2," weighs one hundred and twenty-five pounds, honey colored skin she wears her hair in a honey blonde bob, her lips pierced at the bottom on both sides.

She is sexy and she knows it, but sometimes she lets that shit go to her head.

"I done told yo' hoe ass about that dirty shit." Big Jay gave her a fucked up look. That bitch don't play any games she will kill yo' mama if she gets in her way.

Big Jay is 5'9", two hundred pounds, the color of a Milky Way bar, thick in all the right places, and as rough as she is she doesn't have a mark on her body. Her hair hangs to her shoulders all natural. She is beautiful never wears make-up however she keeps that lip-gloss popping. The girl is flawless, truly a bad bitch.

"Man shut the fuck up." Jasmine yells. Shannon is her baby sister even though they don't often act like it. Nisha is their brother's baby mama. They aren't together anymore but she will always be family for life.

Big Jay is Jasmines' best friend, but the other two love her just as much. Jasmine hates sharing Jay. She acts like she is hers and only hers. That hoe is sick in the head at times. They cursed each other out all the way to Dallas's

spot.

CHAPTER 2

The girls were cursing and fussing with each other so much. They hadn't realized the weather in Saint Louis has gone from a hot summer July day to a cold, dark, and gloomy evening. They pull into the warehouse Dallas owns in Fenton.

The place is huge with all the windows spray painted black so no one could see in or out. The warehouse sits deep back in the woods off interstate 44. Shannon kills the engine to let the car slowly roll into the parking space.

This is the way her sneaky ass always moves. You will never hear her coming but you damn sure going to feel her. Once the car has come to a complete stop the arguing dies instantly. The four women put their game faces on because they know it's not the time to fight with each other, or be cute. Even though they know that sexy is always a requirement when dealing with men.

When they stepped out of the white Chevy Camaro. It looks like a live movie clip of the Fast Five mixed with Charlie's Angles. These bitches are bad. Shannon has on a black wife beater over fishnet leggings with Christian Louboutin Lillian triple buckle black pumps and black D&G sunglasses.

Jasmine has on a black half shirt that read *"Bitches Hate Me"* with black skinny jeans and black Christian Louboutin altadama peep toe platforms.

Big Jay has on an all-black cat suit that hugs her thick body. As if she is wearing liquid latex; she has two skull bone hair clips holding her beautiful hair out of her face, and black Christian Louboutin morphing wedges.

Then there is Nisha who long jet black Remy hair blows in the wind. As she stands there in a black mini dress with an all-black MCM duffle. It's the only kind of bag they used to carry money. Of course she also has on a pair of Christian Louboutin's.

It's a tradition they have with each other. They always wore the same color but in a different style and always the same brand of shoe.

The thunder rolls in the sky as they closed the doors to the car making their way to the building. Nisha leads the way because she is carrying the money and the one that made the promise to Dallas.

Jasmine isn't wild about teaming up with this nigga. She is greedy and already hates splitting the money four ways. Another hand is too much for her to deal with. This time she is gonna trust her friend's judgment. Nisha bangs on the door. A muffled baritone voice says, "I'm coming."

Nisha looks back at her crew as the locks on the other side of the door are heard. Shannon asked, "Y'all ready to die?" Everyone looks at her nodding their heads *"yes"* as they step inside the open door.

They hate when Shannon does this. She always wants them to know shit could get real at any time. She is always ready to die and live at the same damn time.

The room is pretty clean and comfortable to be a warehouse. It has a couch, love seat, coffee table, two plush chairs, and across the way is a sixty-inch flat screen. Dallas has a small office set up with an area rug, desk, computer, high back leather chair, filing cabinets and bookshelves.

Ten men including Dallas are in the room when Nisha and the girls walked up to the desk where D sat. She thought all her girls were by her side until she heard,

"This some bullshit! Nigga why the fuck didn't you cover me?" Shannon is fussing at a sexy caramel colored nigga. That nigga looks like sand on the beach with ocean blue eyes and a sandy red faded Mohawk.

From where she was standing he looks like he is about five eleven, two hundred and ten pounds. He is fine, but that doesn't mean shit to that crazy ass Shannon right now.

"Hold the fuck up! Girl I didn't even ask you to play. You just joined in." He yells.

"So fucking what? Your bitch ass looked as if you needed some help." Shannon is on her feet now.

"Bitch please," he huffed while thinking about how bad this bitch is.

Shannon smiled at him, "Your dick hard ain't it? You want to fuck me don't you?"

"Girl you not all that! So why you asking if my dick hard, girl bye." He tries to walk away.

Shannon side stepped him and jumps right in his face grabbing his dick. It was hard as a jaw breaker. She kissed him "Told you."

CHAPTER 3

Dallas is dying laughing at how this chick has just handled one of his toughest men. The nigga is steaming because he never had a woman make him feel weak and warm inside all at the same time.

"Aye D that shit ain't funny man," he huffs.

"Zane my bad nigga I am not laughing at you, trust me, I am laughing with you." He is still tickled when Nisha chimed in, "I'm back for a reason."

D stopped laughing "What? You couldn't pull the nigga cord could you?" He asks.

"What do you call cord pulling?" Jasmine asked asks getting pissed. He just looks at her wondering if she'd be the first out of this crew to cause him problems.

"I think a shot to the back of the dome and a broken neck covers that." Jasmine boasts because she hates when niggas acted like a bitch couldn't get the fucking job done.

Dallas looks at Nisha like is she bullshitting. Nisha just smiles at him and he shakes his head at what he heard. He has his eye on Jay. The thick teapot is very quiet yet breathtaking.

"Baby you don't talk much do you?" he asks Jay.

"Why do I need to talk when I already have you intrigued with my silence?" she smirks.

Dallas knows that he had gotten himself in a bunch of trouble dealing with these women. He could tell they all are deadly weapons in one way or another. He lays back in his chair pondering the thought.

Nisha broke his train of thought, "Dallas are you going to daydream or get down to business?"

"Show me what you got," he says leaning forward in his chair. Nisha dumps the four hundred grand on his desk causing him to jump up.

"About how much you think that is?" he asks.

"I don't think! I know its four hundred grand," Jasmine told him.

"Four hundred grand? Really?" he asks very impressed with the skills before him. These hoes are goldmine.

"Yeah he was saving up to buy me a million-dollar house, cash money that I told him I wanted." Nisha loves tooting her own horn. "This girl right here makes shit happen." She pats her pussy as she gave credit to it.

Dallas is very interested in the pussy she is carrying to make a nigga grind that hard for her. Then again he thought, some pussy is just better left alone.

"Now that ya'll have made this happen are ya'll ready to join this family? Once you're in there's no turning back." Dallas always let the people that got down with his team know that death is the only way out of this family. He gave them a choice to ride or not. After all, it is a free country.

"Look Dallas, if we didn't want to be here nigga we wouldn't have come. We're holding enough money to keep us pretty cool. Until we decide to make our next move boo" Shannon assures him.

"Lil mama why you so hot headed? Calm the fuck down. We see you boo!" He checks her or so he thought.

"Well that means I'm handling shit all wrong cause I hate to be seen or heard. I'd rather be felt!" She leans in licking the nigga on his lips very gently.

Dallas laughs, "Bitch never lick me like that again in your life. I will kill you before I let you fuck up my mind." The whole room burst into laughter. All the men loved the new women that are about to become a part of their lives.

"We in D just give us our next move. We're on it and will report back to you once we have the money. Even though we work for you if we come across our own lick, we will get that too," Big Jay informs him.

"So what's my cut?" He wants to see where their heads were.

"This money right here you have no cut. This is our lick. We just brought it to show you how we move" Jasmine steps in.

"On the other hand, whatever you find for us your finder fee is a sixty/forty split. The licks we find on our own there's an eighty/twenty split only because we decided to be a part of this family. Hate it or love it, the rates won't change," Nisha told him.

They blowing his mind on so many levels. That he is already starting to fall

in love with each of one them. Shannon
reminds him so much of Keisha. He
knows with these bitches he would have
to lay down the ground rules.

"Ladies I respect all your terms. Now
it's time for you to respect mine." Dallas
looks around to make sure he has their
attention.

"First thing, no matter who finds the
lick, I or you'll, they all should be okayed
by me. I know everything about every
hustler in and outside the STL. It's best
to have background info on the
muthafucka you're about to press. It can

make your shit just a little easier." He pauses to make sure they are feeling him.

"Second, I know that ya'll got heart like a muthafucka but I still want the Duffle Bag Boyz to be back up heat for the Duffle Bag Bitches and vice versa."

Neither the men nor the women are wild about this rule but they have to deal with it.

"Last but never least, if for any reason you come across any of them Vicious or Venom workers, do not, I repeat DO NOT fuck with them. Pass on that lick. We don't need that kind of heat at home. There's bigger fish out here, trust me" Dallas finished.

Shannon spoke, "Vicious and Venom ain't shit! They can get it just like any other muthafucka." She is pissed because she hates those hoes. Their names hold too much weight in the street.

"Feel free to do as you wish baby, just know that me or my crew will not go to war with them because of your ego. If you want your name to hold that kind of weight. You got to put in the work love." As much as she hates what he just said she knows that he is right.

Vicious has been holding her own for some time now. Once she found her twin sister Venom they became the most unstoppable women duo in the Lou. It is all good though because in a matter of time the Duffle Bag Bitches would be known as well.

CHAPTER 4

The ladies left the warehouse feeling like they were on cloud nine. They are about to get money with one of the newest major players in the Lou. Even though he isn't born and bred there you would have thought he was.

Dallas hold his own weight in the city. He is loved by few and hated by many. Things are starting to look up. All the women have a hundred thousand a piece they were sitting lovely.

Nisha planned to use her money for shopping, taking care of her children, and buying herself a ride. She lives with her mother she liked it that way. Her mother take care of the kids most of the time anyway. Nisha is about herself. She wants to party, live the carefree life. Which isn't a bad idea if you have someone in your corner to help you live that way.

Nisha isn't with Jasmine and Shannon's brother Staccz anymore. After years with both of them lying and playing games with each other's hearts. Staccz has finally called it quits. If Nisha had it, her way they would have stayed together forever.

That chance has passed though there was nothing left to do but move on. As Nisha sat in the car with the trio, she is very excited about her new life. She planned to enjoy it to the fullest. From here on out, she is feeling like fuck all niggas. She planned to just get money. Love doesn't live there anymore.

Jasmine sits across from Nisha glancing at her a few times, wondering what she is thinking. Jasmine and her sisters never really cared for Nisha because she is known for lying, but still they love her no matter what. Family is family regardless of their shortcomings.

Jasmine know that she is glad to have this money but she isn't gonna be able to shine or ball out like these hoes. She has four children and a husband. He is a great man and father. Korey stands about five-foot-eight, one hundred seventy-five pounds of muscle, and the color of an Almond Joy.

His dreads hang well pass his shoulders and he has a smile that made you feel as if the doctor is using his light to examine you. Yeah she has some eye candy on her arm. This crazy bitch doesn't play about her nigga either. She would rip your fucking heart out for looking at that nigga too long. Jasmine thinks about how she would have to hide the money. Slowly inch it into her life.

She could never let her husband know that she was out there risking her life. Even if she feels justified doing it. In some ways she is just plain ole greedy when it came to the almighty dollar.

As she sits there, she is already planning to save most of her money because she knows that she won't last long in this new family.

A four-way split is too rich for her blood. They all came into this together with Dallas in their pocket now. She knows that her departure would come sooner rather than later. She really doesn't care for this dude. Jasmine will deal with anything for a small period of time just to make money.

She only has one issue now that she is down with the Duffle Bag Bitches. there is no way out according to Dallas. The thought caused her to chuckle because she doesn't think he knows who he is dealing with.

"What the fuck you laughing at?" Big Jay asks.

"None of your fucking business! Damn!" Jasmine also has a real fucked up attitude.

"Bitch hold the phone and check your email for the bullshit. It just might be coming right back to you." Big Jay is sweet as apple pie but she didn't take no shit from anyone. People often made the mistake of taking her kindness for weakness.

"Bitch it isn't even like that and you know it." Jasmine often talks rough to people but doesn't mean shit by it. Sometimes she doesn't know how harsh she sounds and would become puzzled. When someone became angry with her.

Shannon and Nisha watched the two very close friends bicker with each other. Nisha is still in her own box and couldn't wait to get out of the car to get a move on with the rest of her day. She has shit to do and had enough of these bitches for one day.

Shannon on the other hand is listening to them, she laughs here and there. As always, she has to put her two cents into the conversation. "Jay I don't know why you wasting your breath on her ass. She gonna find a way to be right!" Shannon looks at Jasmine

shaking her head.

CHAPTER 5

Before Jay could respond, Jasmine let loose, "Bitch who asked you to say something? You always got your muthafuckin mouth running like a leaky ass faucet." Jasmine is pissed now. Shannon is her baby sister she always found a way to get under her skin.

"Bitch pump your brakes because this here ain't what you want!" Shannon let her know she is about to get her ass whooped. She is hot headed all the time no matter if she is right or wrong.

"What the fuck you mean this ain't what I want? Bitch you ain't hard. I keep telling your dirty ass that." Jasmine know

she struck a nerve by calling Shannon

dirty.

"Dirty? Bitch please, never! What

the fuck you thinking? I was getting

money before I got down with you hoes

and your little hustle." Shannon always

acts like her shit doesn't stink.

"Just because your ratchet ass did a

little modeling for a book cover? That

don't mean shit to me." Jasmine is kind

of tight about the book cover that

Shannon was on. Their older sister wrote

books she used one of Shannon's

pictures for the cover. Ever since then Shannon feels like she is hot shit for real.

"Your hating ass had to bring that shit up don't you?" Shannon laughs. Jasmine is about to hit her with a comeback, but Jay had enough of their shit already. She is pulling up in front of Nisha's ole birds' crib. She kills the engine Nisha jumps out.

"Aye! Ya'll bitches gone shut the fuck up! I am sick of hearing all this bullshit" Jay fusses.

"Who the fuck you think you are? To tell us to shut the fuck up?" Shannon asks.

"Bitch I am Jay, that's who the fuck I am. I don't want to hear this shit. Plus, ya'll are sisters, so act like it." Jay checks her ass.

"That bitch ain't shit to me!" Jasmine says.

"You right about that. You just mad cause your greedy, hating ass is sitting back there thinking about a way to say fuck the team. Because too many hands in the pot now." Shannon knows her sister too well.

"Bitch you don't know what the fuck you talking about! So you need to fall the fuck back for real." Jasmine is pissed because Shannon has read her mind.

"Jay move the ride so I can get to my crib. Away from this whack hoe." Jasmine hates Shannon at times.

Jay put the car in gear praying that Shannon would just let the conversation go. Her prayers are answered for the time being. She knows they will go back at it sooner or later. She is trying to get Jasmine to her crib as soon as possible.

They made it to Jasmine's spot in no time, Jay is so glad. Shannon is in her own thoughts. Thinking about how she would use her money to plush her crib out. Shop for herself and daughter Jailah, and trick out the Monte Carlo she got a few months ago.

Shannon is excited about working with Dallas. He is hella fine, but that lil nigga Zane. That she was talking shit to is gonna get it with his sexy ass. She loves her sister Jasmine very much. Shannon can't deal with her mouth or selfish ways. She knows it's time to start feeding her with a long handled spoon, family or not.

Jasmine exits the car still pissed off with Shannon. It all fades away when Shannon yells "Love you sis!"

Jasmine looks back at the car, "Love you too bitch." She smiles as she walks away. She loves her family because she was taught to love her own blood no matter what.

Their mom isn't gonna have it any other way. She is the kind of woman that opened her heart and door to anyone in need. She taught her children to do the same. Yet she is also hell in a handbasket. The fire you see blazing in Jasmine and Shannon they inherited it from there mother. She is the living proof of god can change things.

Jay loves the love they have between them. That's why she fucks with them like she does. She drops Shannon off at her crib around the corner from Jasmine's. Now she is finally alone with herself to think. She has a hundred thousand dollars that she could put to great use.

She lives with her mother; Jay know it's time to move on but she isn't ready to live alone. She has no children or a man a few that she tried to show love to. Even though they not worth the air she breathes. She knows this will change one day.

God sees the good in a person no matter how you live your life. He always knows and give your heart desires.

Jay know she will sit on her money stacking it. As they work with this nigga Dallas. He seems cool as a fan. She knows they will end up being great friends real soon. She drives the old beat up car to her peoples' house so he could take it to the chop shop.

CHAPTER 6

Dallas is very impressed with the four women that graced his presence today. He feels that they are perfect for his crew. Plus, he likes having bad bitches around. It makes his day to see a bad bitch put in work like a man. It's the respect that she has for herself to realize that she is more valuable than what is between her legs.

Some women don't know much outside of their pussy. Some even though pussy makes the world go round. The truth of the matter is it really has no more value than a dick.

Niggas get so moved by the feeling that pussy gives them it causes some of them to lose their minds. That's where his girls came in to play. They will lay on a nigga and learn his weakness.

Not all niggas are moved by pussy. Some niggas like loyalty, respect, time, and tenderness. Same bitch, different nigga.

Dallas was born to sell sexuality. He is almost famous for getting money. He is a rare breed not many men can do the things he does. He has a way with women that causes them to love and respect him. He sat in the chair with his squad still in the room watching Zane from afar. He knows the young man's mind is blown by the way Shannon made him feel.

Zane is a player in every way women falling at his feet. He has broken many hearts, so many women love and hates this one man. He wants to love but never found anyone that is worthy. In his eyes they all are the same. They want him for his money or good looks. He hates that because it was never about his character or personality, it's about what he has to offer.

Dallas can tell that his mind is spinning, "Aye! Zane my dude. Why you so quiet over there?" he asks.

"It's nothing fam, thinking that's all." He tries to play it cool, but he isn't fooling Dallas one bit.

"You sure about that pimp?" Dallas asks. As if he doesn't know the answer.

"D why you sweating me?" Zane is becoming irritated. He doesn't like the way he feels. This nigga is all in his ear with some bullshit.

"Damn! Really? Shorty, you in your box about something I done?" Dallas asks. Knowing good and well this shit has nothing to do with him.

"Look man, I'm thinking. You have done shit. I got a lot on my mind," he assures Dallas.

The rest of the squad looks on as the conversation takes place. Dallas can see that his boy not feeling it today he let it go. Dallas begins to address the whole squad, "Listen up. I want ya'll to understand what has happened today. I open the door to a new world of money.

There are only so many places that we as men can get into. When we do enter it's always with force. The four women that came here today will allow us to go places. That we may have never gotten into because as ya'll know you catch more flies with honey," Dallas schools them.

Zane in his box as he explodes, "Man we don't need them hoes! We been doing this shit before they came along. Now we need their help?" He is pissed.

The room is quiet. No one has ever seen him act this way. Dallas on the other hand know what this about. He plays it like a G. "I know how you feel about adding new people to the family.

I'm asking that you trust my judgment this time." The men know the boss doesn't need Zane's approval even though he acts as if he does.

"Whatever! Do what ya'll wanna do. I'm outta here. I've got shit to do!" Zane huffs walking out the door.

The door to the warehouse slams shut. Zane is so hot that he doesn't know what to do with himself. He never felt so funny about working with bitches. He would even pick up money from the prostitutes that works for Dallas.

Zane in his feelings because this too much for him to take in. This woman is probably not tripping off what he is doing. So he wondering why he can't get her off his mind.

He starts his car; the radio is playing "*Words*" by Bobby V. This song is his jam, but today it's too much. He can't believe these emotions lives inside of him.

Something about this woman had has awaken something inside of him that been dead for so long. Zane know nothing about love. He has been on his own since he was ten years old. His mother was mentally ill; his father just didn't give a fuck. Zane was often hungry, dirty, beaten, and cold. He was the baby of his family.

His older brothers and sisters went on with their lives. As soon as they could, never bothering to look back to see if he needed anything. Zane begins hustling at the tender age of thirteen. There is no other way for him to survive in the jungle.

By the time he was sixteen, he was making ten thousand a week that was just the start of his hustling. Now he brought in fifty to a hundred grand a week. He has never loved any bitch in his muthafuckin life. He damn sure isn't about to start now.

CHAPTER 7

Nisha is on cloud nine with the little hundred thousand dollars. She is splurging bought a new car, clothing, and got her hair done. A few things for the children gave her mom a little piece of change to keep her off her back.

Nisha bragging a lot about how she is getting money. All her little girlfriends want to be down. She lies to them saying that she will look out for them. Knowing good and damn well that shit isn't happening. She likes to make muthafuckas think she has them.

Truth be told, now that the squad is working for Dallas. She nor any of the others run shit. Nisha will soon learn this. She is enjoying the little bit of money that she has left. However, she is starting to run low. It's time to look for a new lick.

She decides it's time to call her girls. Shannon picks up the phone dialing Jasmine's number. The phone rings for a minute. "Hello," Jasmine says into the phone.

"Bitch what's good with you boo?" Nisha says cheerfully.

"Shit, at home with my family."
Jasmine is always iffy.

"Aye we need to contact Dallas about a new lick. We need to hit the club to find out who's holding that paper." Nisha says.

"What the fuck you mean?" Jasmine looks around the room. Remembering that she is in the room with her husband and kids. She is about to yell out how much money Nisha has. She looks at her husband, *"Baby this dumb bitch Nisha. I'm gonna take this in the other room. So I won't mess up ya'll movie."* He shakes his head. She exits the room ready to blow this bitch down.

"Please tell me that you haven't spent all that money Nisha!" Jasmine hates when people wastes money.

"I got about ten bands left." She says that shit like it's cute.

"You spent that much fuckin money on what? I hear you are out there bragging about the money you getting. I know you not that stupid." Jasmine's mind is blown.

"What the fuck you got to do with how I spend my fuckin money? Hell, I should have got more than everyone else!

I was the one fuckin the ugly ass lame nigga, not you hoe." Nisha is pissed because she hates when people calls her stupid. Even though she knows it's true.

"Bitch if you don't pump your muthafuckin brakes. We're gonna have a fuckin issue." Jasmine grits her teeth because she is trying to change her life and her temper.

"Look, are ya'll ready to get this money because we don't have time to be sitting on this little bit of money. No fuckin way! We trying to be rich!" Nisha sounds stupid saying that. Knowing that she has fucked up her money.

"I'm gonna holla at the girls tonight. See where their heads are. You're just gonna have to play it easy with your ten little bands." Jasmine laughs hanging up. She has to admit this stupid bitch is funny at times.

Jasmine calls Shannon. "Hey sis," Shannon says as she picks up.

"Hell wish I was as happy as you" Jasmine states. This makes Shannon wonder why her sister is unhappy. When she has everything she could ask for. A husband to love her crazy ass no matter what. She has four beautiful children one girl three boys

Now they are getting money, besides lying to a great man. Shannon can't put her finger on the issue at all. Out of love she asks, "What's the matter boo?"

"Nothing sis. I told you I'm getting help for myself to save my family." Jasmine is serious Shannon that quality in her.

"Well then bitch what's good with it?" That causes Jasmine to laugh. She knows they don't get along at times. When they do, Shannon can be a damn fool.

"Man are you ready to hit another lick. I think we need to lay low for a

while. They still looking for West's killer."
Jasmine is shook knowing that she is the
person they are in search of.

"Sis it's no rush for me. I'm still
holding seventy-five so I am Gucci for
real." Shannon told her.

"Aye man, click over and call Jay."
Shannon doesn't know what Jasmine is
tripping off. Because she knows that her
sister doesn't waste money like that.
Shannon does what she is ask to do.

Jay must be on the phone because
Shannon had to dial her line a few times
before she got her. "Shannon what the
hell you blowing my damn phone up for?

With your skinny crack head ass?" Jay loves to talk shit. She is a Cancer that's what they do.

"Bitch your momma a crack head," Shannon jokes. Even though she knows that Jay doesn't play games about her damn momma.

"Hoe fuck you with yo fluffy ass momma. Why the fuck you calling me to play games?" Jay loves this girl, crazy and all.

"Hey bitch, don't talk about our momma fluffy like your ass slim!" Jasmine and Shannon both double teams her ass.

"Oh let me find out this some tag team shit!" Jay laughs at their silly asses.

"No ya'll, for real, let's cut the bullshit. Ya'll ready to do another lick or what?" Jay is just as shocked as Shannon is at the words coming out of Jasmine's mouth.

She knows how her best friend is with money. Jay wonders where this is coming from. "You broke Jazz?"

"Hell no, you know fuckin better than to ask me some shit like that." Jasmine almost got pissed but she plays it cool.

"Well why the hell are you asking us this?" This time Jay and Shannon are on the tag team mission.

"Man this bitch Nisha is down to ten bands." Jasmine says shaking her head like they could see her.

"Ten bands!" Both yells. As if their ears are playing tricks on them.

"Yeah! She calls me with her chest poked out. Talking about how she should have gotten more money than the rest of us. Because she was the one fuckin the nigga" Jasmine informs them of their conversation.

"Fuck that ratchet ass bitch! She better be glad that she not fuckin broke." Jays says

"For real like she was before my brother started fuckin with her dumb ass." Shannon is pissed at the balls of that bitch.

"I know that shits right sis" Jay says. She doesn't like to do a lot of talking. Jay rather fuck you up.

"I know ya'll think its bitch fault, but she family and we can't let the hoe dry up." Jasmine says. Jay and Shannon can't believe this shit. The next move was evening more shocking.

"Fuck it! I'll call Dallas when we hang up see what he holding for us." Jay never jump starts shit. They are wondering what is moving her.

"Really?" Jasmine and Shannon are back on the tag team.

"Yeah I will handle it. Unless one of ya'll want to do it" Jay says, ready to pass the torch because this isn't her thing.

"No, do your thang boo. Tell us what we got to do." Shannon says.

They all said "One Luv!" hanging up.

Jay doesn't think twice about what she just did. It is what it is, now or never for her to step up to the plate making it happen. Even if its Nisha's dumb ass that

needing money so soon.

CHAPTER 8

Ring... Ring... Ring... Dallas is an early bird to have his hand in so much shit. Its barely nine fifteen the nigga is in the bed. "Hello," he whispers in a low sexy voice. That made you think he is doing one of two things. Jay calling about business she pushes that shit to the back of her mind.

"Hey D, this Jay the silent killer!" This causes him to laugh and wake up a little more.

"What's up boo? What's the cause for you to awaken me in such a lovely way?" Boy does this man have a way with words I tell you.

"It's like this, we need to come see you. If you feeling where I'm coming from" she speaks in code.

"Ya'll bringing one to me or ya'll need one from me?" he asks. So he could tell her what her next moves are.

"No we need one because we didn't plan to have to come back this fast. Some shit came up and here we are." Jay put him on game.

"If that's the case tell Shannon to give Zane a call. Tell him to give her details on the latest one we laying on.

Now he's kind of a hard cookie to crack. We gonna need something hot to move this one. You might just fit the bill. Thick, chocolate, and fine; shit, you would have me open." Dallas causing Jay to blush. A part of her likes it but the other part doesn't.

"That's what it does then. If the role calls for me to be the leading act, then I'm willing to ride for my family. Let's see what Zane got on this cat first, ya dig." Jay flips game back at him not knowing loves this shit. Strong women drive Dallas wild.

"I dig shorty" he says, hitting her with southern swag.

"Sleep tight daddy, we eating' in the morning!" That statement made Dallas's dick hard. "Opps my bad," Jay shocks herself when she said it he laughs.

"Will do shorty." Dallas smiles

He is happy that he added the girls to the crew. Things will work just the way he needs them to. If everyone is smart, within five years they will all be able to retire at very young ages.

Shannon got the word from Jay to call Zane. She did as she is asked. When she called, the nigga is acting crazy talking about *"How did you get this number?"* This nigga acting like she a stalker or some shit. Shannon didn't sweat it. Whatever wrong with him he will soon get over.

This about business, nothing more. After Zane gives her the information need. They don't have to speak again as far as she is concern.

Zane wasn't willing to talk over the phone. Shannon cool with that because she isn't feeling that phone shit either. He asks her to meet him at *The Melting Pot* in *Delmar Loop*. It's a fondue restaurant in University City better known as U City. Shannon is feeling that because she loves to eat. Even though she was a skinny Minnie. A fat woman lives within.

She walks into the place with her black Levi skinny jeans, a grey Levi wife beater Shannon tops the outfit off with a Pave bow wish necklace, bracelet, heart studs and delight glitter heels, all by Juicy Couture. This bitch is causal but still the shit.

You don't always have to be Gucci, Louie, & Prada to make a statement.

Simple bitches live by labels are Shannon's view. A real bitch can make herself look good if she shops at the Goodwill. That's what real bitches do! It's called working with what the fuck you got. Instead of buying shit that they can't afford.

Zane is at the table he reserved for them. He feels like he is on a blind that Dallas set up for him without his permission. With an ugly bitch that he told him that he isn't feeling. He knows that isn't the case, Shannon fine as hell.

Zane doesn't want to be bothered with this bitch because her swag is a million. It drives him crazy. No matter how hard he tries to stop thinking about this bitch he can't.

"Hey my dude!" Shannon let him know that she is there.

"Ugh, what's up?" Zane lifts his head hating to look at her. She so fabulous.

"What's the matter boy? If you tired you could have met me in the morning," Shannon says. As she pulls her seat out to sit down. He watches her body movement as if its singing his favorite love song. He hates the way this woman controls his mind without even trying.

"I'm good boo, I'm just…" Zane doesn't know what to say. She has him speechless.

"Well anyway you look good tonight." Shannon smiles at him. As if she has known him all her life. She is right though. Zane fine tonight he sporting a light gray perforated suede racer jacket, sleek black MK shirt, Astor distressed jeans, and white oversized PU chronograph watch all from Michael Kors. The sneakers are Roberto Cavalli. The boy has it going on most definitely getting money.

Shannon is hungry. "What are we eating?" She looks at the menu then at him. "I know this isn't a date but you paying right?" she asks as she looks over the menu at him.

Zane looks at her shaking his head laughing. "Yeah I got us," he says before he knows it. Her experiences taught her that men were afraid of words like *"us"* and *"we"* because it meant oneness.

"I mean I got you." Zane corrects himself quickly.

Shannon looks at him weird. "Boy you strange!" She went on with her order having the shrimp and sirloin plate.

Succulent white shrimp paired nicely with teriyaki-marinated sirloin with vegetable medley in addition to a white wine spritzer.

Zane has the Pacific Rim. All-natural breast of chicken, teriyaki-marinated sirloin, succulent white shrimp, and citrus-infused pork tenderloin, breast of duck and chicken and vegetable pot stickers with red wine.

CHAPTER 9

They were making small talk while they ate their food when Zane asks "Why ya'll need money so fast again?" He wonders what kind of women his crew is dealing with.

"Dang your nosey boy," Shannon jokes.

"I'm curious! I am no boy, girl! I am a man." Zane checks her she looks at him seriously for the first time. He likes having her attention. It made him feel as if he has the upper hand now.

"Well if you must know, one bitch in our crew fucked most of her money on stupid shit. So we back in the field ready to play this game," she says him. Thinking about how she would have loved to chill for a minute.

"That's some bullshit! We going have to have Dallas talk to her about his plans for this crew." Zane is pissed because he hates stupid bitches.

"What plan?" Shannon isn't aware of any plan.

"Don't worry boo, it's all for your good, trust me." He touches her hand.

"I can't do that. I have to wait to see what Dallas say before I trust anything." She is serious.

"Damn, you out to dinner with me but you don't trust me." Zane is kind of hurt. Even though he doesn't know these hoes. He would never hurt one of them.

Shannon see the hurt on him. "Oh no! Baby it's not you. I don't trust men period! I my heart been broken too many times," she told him honestly.

Zane looks at her seeing the hurt in her eyes. There is something inside of him yelling save her! The other part says fuck her. Hell my own mother or sisters never saved me! He can't think of one bitch in his life that actually loves him.

Zane can remember bitches that said they loved him. Once a nigga with more money comes along them hoes love level dropped to zero. So no, he isn't gonna save this woman.

"Aye you quiet, let's get down to business." Shannon is full and missing her daughter.

"My bad babe. It's this lame ass nigga name Cash in South Carolina. He's a bitch but he holding for real. The nigga brings in half a million every week," Zane informs her.

"So why haven't ya'll moved on him?" Shannon wants to know.

"He's bitch happy! Won't let any outside niggas in his crew. That's why D starts looking for a female crew to add to our family. Baby here you are." Zane smiles at her.

Shannon is glad to be a part of the crew she smiles at him. The smile causes him to look away.

"When do we move?" she asks.

"Well you, Jay, and me, we move tomorrow evening," Zane schools her.

"What? Why?" Shannon isn't ready to leave her baby."

"We have the information we need to know about him. We need Jay to move in on him. He likes fluffy women she's what the doctor ordered. D asks her who she wants with her she chose you.

The other two will show up when it's time to move with the rest of the crew.

Shannon slams her body back in her chair, "Let's do it." Zane can tell she is angry about something. He knows it's not money. Looking at how she is decked out tonight.

"What's the matter boo?" Zane hates the words as they left his mouth. You could hear that he cares by his tone.

"It's nothing, I wanted to spend more time with my baby girl. I will make it up to her when I get back." Shannon talks more to herself. Than him as she gets out of her seat preparing to go.

"Aww you got a baby? How old is she mama?" Zane loves kids. He doesn't have any because he wants to be a part of the child's everyday life. He has never loved any woman to stay around that long.

"She's two years old" Shannon says heading for the door.

Zane finds himself following her after throwing a hundred-dollar tip on the table. "Why you doing this love? Why do you risk your life? Knowing you got a beautiful baby girl that needs you?" Zane wants to understand her.

"No nine to five will prevent us from starving," Shannon says as she gets in her car driving away.

Zane watches her with amazement in his eyes. He has fallen in love at that very moment. There is nothing that he could do to stop it. Zane has to figure out a way to handle it.

CHAPTER 10

Shannon rides home thinking about that gorgeous man.

I bet he a player, got hella women and think he all that! Then again he acts like he is caring and sweet person. Why do I care anyway?

He's not my man it's not like he tried to hit on me, he just asked about my baby. Or he could have been doing that to see if he could hit.

Whatever! I am not about to trip off this man anyway. I told myself that I am gonna play it cool be single.

When Shannon got home, her baby and roommate were asleep. She tip-toes into her baby's room kissing her.

"I'm leaving to go out of town in the morning. I promise I am coming back to you. I love you Jailah."

"I love you too mommy." She was still asleep when she said it. Shannon wants to cry, but it's not the time. She will cry when she makes it back.

Shannon takes a bath heading to bed. It's time to put her game face on.

Zane snatches the phone off the hook wondering who is calling his house phone. "What?" he yells, still sleeping.

"You should be getting ready to head to the airport. You know your flight leaves before the girls. I want you to have things in order when they get there," D reminds him.

"Good looking out man, I'm getting my ass up now." Zane begins to move his hard body around. This fine muthafucka even has on Michael Kors boxer briefs.

"How did your date, I mean meeting with Shannon go?" D has to laugh at himself. He knows damn well what he has done. After losing Keisha he never wants anyone to miss out on what he loss. Sometimes men can get in their own way like women tend to do.

"First of all it wasn't a date! She hella cool, she got a baby girl. Shannon isn't ready to leave town so soon. Yet she is built for it so she'll be alright" Zane says shaking his head. Even though no one was there to see him.

"Good. Sounds like a winner." D is trying to pick his brain on his feelings.

"Whatever! I got shit to do so I'll fuck with you later." Zane hangs up on his friend. That is laughing out loud now.

Zane walks to the shower. He lives in Clayton at the Park Condo's on Bonhomme Avenue. The place is breath taking. It featured floor-to-ceiling windows with an amazing view of the city. High vaulted ceilings, luxury plank flooring in the living area, walk-in closets, and a stunning master bathroom.

It measured twelve by twenty-four feet covered with the most expensive porcelain money could buy. The kitchen is equipped with stainless steel GE appliances, granite countertops, a breakfast bar, maple cabinets, and top of the line washer and dryer duo.

He lives very well also very smart with his money. Zane knows what it's like to be poor he never wants to live like that again. He sees that D would have to teach Nisha how to make her money work for her. As taught him.

If he hadn't, Zane would be broke as shit right now. Because he always wanted to stunt hard. He wastes money on clothes, shoes, and other bullshit. He didn't even have a place to stay. Laying up with women in hotels or one of his backstabbing homeboy's house.

Today he paying three thousand dollars a month for his bills, not including his car note. That is another story. He pushing a 2016 Cadillac Escalade Hybrid with a gold mist metallic paint job. The interior is cocoa with full leather seats. He completes the look with twenty-two inch, seven spoke chromed aluminum wheels.

Riding this good costs, him about a G a month. Now that his money is working for him he doesn't even feel the pain. If there is any pain, it's not having anyone he could share it with.

As he drove to the airport, his phone begins to ring. He has it on drive mode the call came through his speakers. To answer, all he had to do is speak.

"Hello." He doesn't know who the hell it is. Zane doesn't save numbers in his phone often. It's only a few people that he feels are important enough to be lock in. The current caller isn't one of them.

"You ain't got time for me right?" Zane knows the voice.

"Tammy, I don't have time for this bullshit today." This is one of his steady pieces of ass. That wants to believe she is his woman. No matter how many times he told her she isn't.

"So you don't have time for your woman?" She asks.

"You're not my woman! I shouldn't have to keep telling you this man." Zane hates to say. Yet he always keeps it real with women. So they can't say shit like *"You using me for sex nor why you cheating on me?"*

"It's like that with us now?" She is starting to wonder because he hasn't touched her in two months.

"It's not like shit! I am doing me; so do you love." Zane always told her that because he knows that he isn't on it like that.

"What? Am I not fine enough for you?" She always tries to make that the reason. Even though it's not the truth. She fine five-feet-five, one hundred and thirty-five pounds, with deep chocolate skin, and natural hazel eyes. If he was on it she would most def fit the bill. Tammy doesn't move him.

"Baby that's not it you fine than a muthafucka for show," he assures her.

"Aww thanks daddy. I miss you." Tammy ate that shit up. He is telling the truth yet it's what turns him off about her. He has to validate her, instead of her knowing it and living her life no matter what he does

"Aye let me call you back. I'm heading on a business trip. I got another call coming in" he told her.

"Let me find out you taking some bitch on a trip!" Tammy is fussing again.

"Get off my phone because you about to piss me off." He wants to get rid of her.

"Sorry...." She doesn't get to finish her statement he hung up.

CHAPTER 11

"Hello!" He yells as he pulls into the airport.

"Hey Zane this..." he cuts her off.

"What's good Shannon?" She is shock that he knows her voice.

"Oh nothing wondering what time we're supposed to be at the airport." Shannon says.

"Damn I meant to call you. I'm heading out now. Ya'll will be flying out about ten in the morning tomorrow." It had slipped his mind.

"Oh my bad for bothering you. I thought you said today." She feels like she isn't paying attention when he was giving her the order.

"No it's cool. I changed it because you need to spend more time with your baby. This short notice too fast for you. I told D I would go get the rooms in order. Ya'll could move in the morning." He says

"Aww! Thank you so much. You didn't have to do that; I know this is business." She wants him to know she is about that life.

"You're right, this is business. What you have with your daughter is love. Cherish it because some of us don't have that." Zane always let his mouth get away from him. When he talks to this woman. She was about to say something. Zane can't bear to talk to her anymore.

"Look boo I got a plane to catch." Just like that he is gone. Shannon looks at the phone speechless when it begins to ring "Hello."

"Bitch what's wrong with you?" Jasmine asks.

"Nothing! There's been a change in the plans. We're not leaving until tomorrow. We need to link up for lunch and talk this shit over." She is still tripping off Zane.

"Cool let's go to 54th St. because that's Jay shit." Jasmine loves her friend.

"I'm always down to eat." They ended the call.

Jasmine always wants to know where her baby sister's head is. She wants the best for her. Jasmine don't know how to express that without being nosey or bossy. Shannon to become angry with her for these reasons. Even though its done out of love. Jasmine almost lost Shannon when she had her baby.

Shannon was in a coma with tubes everywhere, and her lungs even collapsed. That scared the shit out of Jasmine. So she always wants to know that Shannon is okay. That's what big sisters are for

They met at the restaurant at two o'clock. Shannon, Nisha, and Jay sipped Strawberry Long Islands as Jasmine had the Berry Sangria.

This damn girl is crazy about Sangrias. Nisha is always the first to start talking shit when she drinking. That's why muthafuckas don't fuck with her the long way.

"I am shining on these hoes so hard. They ready to get down with the team."

Nisha smiles like muthafuckas feeling the shit that fell out her fucking face.

Jay just looks at the bitch some type of way because she hates stupidity. Shannon looks at her funny as well. Thinking this hoe is the reason she has to leave town so soon.

"Bitch shut the fuck up with your dumb ass. We are Gucci with the money we made! Thinking we wouldn't have to move for at least six months. Your thirsty ass fucked up your money. If you weren't family, yo ass would be dead out here for real." Jasmine is pissed thinking about the risk she is taking. She has a husband and kids to think about.

"Well damn ya'll holding on to that little bit of money! As if you can take it with you!" Nisha tries to make her decision sound good.

"We can't take it with us! We can enjoy it while we're here. If we don't play Russian Roulette with our lives as much as you want us to. This shit a death sentence at any time for any of us. We try to hit major players! So we can do this less often." Shannon schools her ass real fast.

"Hell, if it wasn't for me ya'll wouldn't have shit to hold on to! Am I correct?" Nisha is feeling herself.

"You're partially correct. You fucked the nigga I killed him. Let's not get shit twisted around here. Every hoe got a John, you dig! So don't flatter yourself man." Jasmine bites her head off taking a piece of her ego.

"I am the bitch D and the DBB kidnapped to get money out of West!" Nisha says like she is hurt.

"You are also the same bitch. That had him killed after he proved his love to you! What you want a cookie? Bitch please!" Jay says.

"You also the bitch that's causing us to have to go back in a war zone. I'm glad it's out of town cause shit still hot around here with West's investigation is going strong. His brother Nick Beam won't let the shit rest.

"Fuck Nick Beam, he isn't no damn body! He just wants to be West. Most of all he wants to fuck me!" Nisha is getting scared because she knows how Beam loved his brother.

"I have to beg to differ on the whole fucking thang! All his women are thick or fluffy your crack head skinny. He doesn't want you" Jay told her flat out.

Nisha was about to speak when Shannon's phone begins to ring. She doesn't know the number. That made her not want to pick up! Yet something said she should. "Who dis?" she barks into the phone.

He laughs she knows the tone, "Zane. I am just calling to let you know that ya'll plane leave tomorrow at noon." He is trying to keep from stuttering.

"Two questions," Shannon says. The girls wondering who she is talking to.

"Shoot baby, anything for you!" Zane is kicking himself because he is doing it again. He doesn't know what it is about this woman that causes him to care.

It made Shannon smile. "Why is the flight leaving at noon instead of in the a.m. as you said earlier?" She wonders if everything is good.

"Shit, to allow you more time with your baby. I told D your situation he stated to do whatever I want to handle that for you! So I made the flight leave at noon." He doesn't understand why the way she loves her baby moves him.

Maybe cause his mother never loved him like that.

Shannon plays it cool even though this man is melting her heart. "Good looking out, I dig that. Why you calling me from a strange number? Instead of the one I have saved." She thinks he is trying to be sneaky.

"Babe that's my personal number. Nobody really calls that line but D and a few of my niggas. I don't have much family and I-I-I-I," Zane stutters, "Just thought it would be cool for you to have it. Since we working together, that's all love." Dammit, the more he talks to her the more and more he hates this woman.

Got him stuttering and shit he stop doing

that in the sixth grade.

CHAPTER 12

"Aye look, let me get you off my phone. I got shit to do." Zane tries to be mean on purpose. Acting as if she is getting on his nerves. Shannon driving him insane in a great way.

"Oh cool it's like that huh?" Shannon is confused by his change of tone. She doesn't take it to heart though.

"Yeah it is." It kills him to tell that lie.

"Well bye" Shannon fussed.

"Bye!" He looks at the smiling.

Shannon hangs up the phone feeling some type of way the expression registered all over her face.

"Who the hell was that?" Jasmine aka Ms. Nosy has to ask.

"If you must know that was Zane calling about business" she barks.

"Business my ass!" Jay chimes in. Nisha and Jasmine burst out laughing.

"No for real, Zane was telling me our flight leaves at noon." Shannon tries to redeem herself.

"Girl that boy has you open like a vodka bottle in a room full of drunks,"

Jasmine said says. She has to admit happiness looks good on her sister.

"He does not!" Shannon is becoming angry. Everyone saw it so they let it go. They plan to watch this shit unfold.

"So when we leaving?" Nisha's hot ass is ready to roll.

"You aren't going no damn where just yet! This job requires me and Shannon's expertise at the present time. So fall your ass back" Jay told her.

"Yeah, ya'll will arrive the day before we make the move with the rest of the crew" Shannon assures her.

"I hope this little money I got last until this shit goes through," Nisha states like someone cared.

"If it doesn't that's on you!" Jasmine says The trio burst out laughing exiting the restaurant.

Morning came too damn fast it seems as if Shannon had just closed her eyes. However, her she is with Jay going to the airport. She enjoys the extra time Zane gave her too but it wasn't enough. Shannon has the same hope as Nisha for this shit to be over soon but for a different reason.

They are heading to Lambert Airport getting ready to fly out to Columbia, South Carolina. Jay planned to pick up Shannon, as she fumbling around trying to get ready.

Jay truly isn't a morning person but she knows that today she had to be up early to make this flight on time. She doesn't even bother to pack her bags! She will shop when she got there as a pastime.

Plus, since she is the type of lady this man loved, she has to make it do what it does. Now that her time to shine has finally come.

She went out the door when her phone begins to ring. Shannon is calling. She thought her friend was calling to press her for running a few minutes late.

"What you want hooker?" Jay chimes when she answers the phone.

"Aye, did you get picked up by car service?" she asks.

"No I am in my car." Jay is confused now.

"Well head to the airport. I don't know what's going on. I will see you when I get there." Shannon hang up still confused.

Shannon sitting inside the 2016 Lincoln. She is loving the ride even though she doesn't know why she is in it. She doesn't know D that well. Why would he send a car for her and not Jay? That isn't his swag by far. Its more to this but she going to enjoy the ride for now.

Jay is waiting at the C concourse for Shannon. So they could board the plane together. Shannon is running down the concourse to make sure she wouldn't miss the flight. She was so comfortable in the luxury ride that she dosed off.

Shannon isn't sure why she got the star treatment. She needed it and could definitely get used to it.

She wants to think about the why and how! Shannon doesn't have time. Right now it's time to put her game face on. When you go in the zone you have to always be ready for war. She would think about luxuries when she got back home.

Jay sees Shannon running her way. She yells, "Over here!" Shannon follows her voice with her ticket in hand. When she got close to Jay she says "Wait!" she is scared.

"What's up sis?"

"I'm scared! I never been on a plane before." She has fear in her eyes that Jay has never seen before.

"Me either, but look at it this way - we're flying first class. If we die we'll be together going out in style," Jay smiles.

"You ready to die?" Shannon asks her.

"Yeah let's ride." She grabs her hand boarding the plane.

The flight was smooth it took only a few hours to get there. The girls enjoyed their first plane ride. Delta Airlines first class is the shit. It made you feel as if you are riding in a spaceship.

The complimentary food and drink aren't bad either. By the time the plane landed, the girls are in la-la land. They touched down at Columbia Owens downtown airport.

CHAPTER 13

They aren't sure what the next move is until they see a man dressed in chauffeur's attire waving a *DBB* sign. That's their cue.

"Are you our driver?" Shannon asks.

"Are you ladies the Duffle Bag Bitches?" he asks. As if he has been dying to meet them all day.

"Yes we are." Jay smiles.

"Follow me please." The two women follows behind the driver. They are blown away than suddenly they realized. That they are no longer small time. They are in the big leagues now.

They have signed up for some real shit. They have to be ready for it. The limousine pulls up to 700 Woodrow St. The Whitney Hotel. Shannon and Jay heads to the desk where the receptionist looks to be engaged in a more personal than professional telephone call.

She acts as if she doesn't see them. Jay clears her throat which caused the lady to end her call.

"Yes, what might I be able to help you with? If you need directions or to use the rest room, we don't allow that here." Shannon looks at Jay like can you believe this bitch.

"The limo parked out front dropped us off here. So I would think you were expecting us" Shannon told her.

She looks over at the pearl white limo that Mr. Thomas had specifically asked for. He is a valued customer that often came to their place of business. Among other things she knows him personally. She looks back at the two women.

"I see you're the guests that Zane Thomas reserved a room for," she states. They don't know Zane's last name but hell, who else could she be talking about.

Their thoughts are broken by "My name is..." Shannon cut her wind off.

"We don't care to know your name! One thing we do know is that you're rude as hell! So with that being said I assume that most people call you bitch. We just need to know where are sleeping." Shannon is now standing in the fighting stance with her hand on her hip.

Jay is dying laughing at the look on the bitch face. She passed the key card that read 314. It is usually the room Zane stayed in. It made him feel at home. He wants them to feel the same way. He took the room across the hall, 315.

The room is very warm and spacious with a modern day décor. It's a two-bedroom suite equipped with a living room, full kitchen, and a washer and dryer. To top it all off it came with 24-hour limousine service. It's a great place to lay low when you know in a week's time shit is going to get real.

No more laying on niggas for months at a time. Two weeks' tops to learn everything about their day to day lives. Then move in on 'em taking what they wanted. The girls were chilling in the room talking when they hear a knock at the door. Shannon know its Zane, so she opens the door without asking who it is.

Zane walks in with another man that is sexy as hell. "Girl why you open the door? You don't know who could be watching!" he fusses thinking these bitches ain't cut out for this shit.

"Boy, shut the fuck up!" Shannon told him.

"For real! What if someone found out you are in town?" Zane asks.

"I'm gonna lay 'em down." Shannon looks him in his eyes while lifting her shirt to show him the four five she is holding.

The coca colored man is laughing. He loves this woman's G even though it's his first time meeting her.

"Man shut your ass up." Zane says to the man then introduce him. "This is Mack he works with the crew too. He wasn't at the warehouse when you joined the family." Mack six foot one, a basketball build, deep black wavy hair, and golds on each of his fang teeth. Baby boy is fire that's for show'.

"Hey Mack. I'm Shannon this is Jay." Jay waves from across the room. While she lay on the couch smoking trees.

"Nice to meet you ladies." Mack looks over at Jay. "Can I hit that?" he asked.

Jay doesn't play about her weed. "You ain't put in on this man." She is so serious. Shannon and Zane are dying laughing.

"Stingy ass!" Mack is pissed because he wants to smoke.

"Bitch ass nigga, I ain't stingy, I just like to smoke alone every once in a while. I'll sell you some though." Zane is looking at her like she is crazy! Before Mack could say anything,

"How the hell you get weed on a plane?" Zane wants to know because they used to be sick when they were here on their stakeouts. The shit they sold down here is like smoking grass seeds.

Mack doesn't let Jay respond, "Fuck that, give me a dub?" She whipped it out of her titties handing him the trees. As she grabbed the money!

"Now back to my question" Zane chimes back in.

"In my pussy!" Jay says still smoking.

Mack smelling the bag. He looks up at Shannon and Zane watching him, "This shit smell fire," he says.

They both begin to laugh again. Shannon dies laughing when Zane said, "We gone call this TittyPuss." This causes Mack and Jay to join in the laughter.

CHAPTER 14

The family is growing closer. They are heading to a club tonight. That's the reason for the men's' visit. They came to tell them to be looking right tonight. They have a week days to make shit happen and get back home, but the sooner the better.

The women had car service to pick them up. So they can get what they needed to make the night count. Sometimes you only get one time to make shit right. That's the plan to gain this nigga's trust in a small time frame. If your game is right, it can be done within the first fifteen minutes of conversation.

The women had the car take them to Columbiana Centre Mall. Its located in the heart of Columbia, South Carolina on Harbison Blvd. The mall has every store you could imagine. The girls know they are going to enjoy themselves.

The duo walks in the mall like they owned the place. They have their boss's black card everything is on him. They don't need to spend one dime The new crew is about to spoil them.

They couldn't decide on what they want to hit first! Charlotte Russe, Buckle,

Love Culture, New York & Company, or Reeds Jewelers. They had lunch at Schooners, one of the best places to eat in Columbia. Not too far from the mall or the hotel. The food is off the meter.

Jay and Shannon wants to sit and chill before everything takes place. They know after today its gonna be work from there on out.

Jay looks at Shannon. "How you feel about the lick and our new crew?" She needs to know.

"I think it's going to work out for real. I can see that we will be well taken care of. I know it's new but we can handle this boo." Shannon feeling the love coming from her new family.

"Yeah your right sis. I'm tripping. Maybe because this the first time I have to be the one to lure the bitch nigga in," Jay laughs.

"Bitch all you got to do is blow his mind tonight. The end of the week we running up in there taking everything. They say he a stunner so this is gonna be easy! Like taking candy from a baby!" Shannon smiles at her.

"Damn right! Let's eat bitch so we can get this money!" Jay loves her bestie Shannon. They ordered their food.

Shannon has the fish tacos and Jay enjoyed a soft shell crab BLT.

They conversed a little more, paid the bill than set off to make that money. Little did they know shit is about to get real.

Night came its time to get a move on. The ladies are getting ready. They hurried trying to get it together. So that they wouldn't keep the men waiting. They still were taking too long because the knocking at the door came again.

Shannon swing the door open. She is practically dressed Jay is still in the shower. Zane was with Mack he was about to start fussing at her again. But she has him speechless.

Shannon is standing there in a black bra and thong from Victoria Secret's. Her body is banging. The two men standing there as if they were fools until she says, "Ya'll coming in or going to let everyone in the hotel see my ass?" They both move slowly because they couldn't take their eyes off of her.

"I'll be ready in a minute, just got to go slip on my dress." She talks to them. As if she is fully clothed nun. The men are sin a trance when Jay came out the bathroom fully clothed.

"What is wrong with you niggas? Damn, sit down somewhere, we coming!" she says. That bitch is on her "A" game. She is wearing a zip back black and cream lace corset with liquid zip legged leggings from Charlotte Russe.

The zebra platform pumps with black and pearl accessories set it off. Jay shoulder length hair is flawless with skull hair bows topping it off. The outfit hugs her thick body very well. The men are thinking this shit is a wrap.

"This nigga Cash is going to melt at the sight of this bitch." Mack thought.

Shannon came hauling ass out of the room. "I'm ready." She is wearing a red and black millennium peplum dress, red accessories, and vampire-collar velvet pumps.

These bitches are so fly you couldn't tell if they are going on a date or mission for the crew. The four of them set out to make this easy money.

The crew entered PT 1109 as if they owned the place. Its packed with niggas and bitches. This place is bringing in a nice piece of money. Zane know it's a front for some nigga's hustle.

Lucky for him he is not the target that night. Mack and Zane went to mingle with the ladies. As Shannon and Jay worked the room. The place is huge. VIP is on the second level showcasing a glass balcony that looks down on the lower level.

Cash is sitting in the middle because he wants to see everyone that came in and out of the club while he is there.

Cash is about five foot eight, two hundred and fifty pounds with cocoa brown skin, and dressed impeccably. He is kind of on the chubby side but not what you would call fat. He is one of the most paid niggas out there on the street grind. The man is making moves pulling in about three hundred thousand a week. He stunts a little but not enough for a new nigga to get into his circle.

He is bitch happy cause he didn't get many women when he was younger due to his weight. It wasn't until he became the man that bitches started throwing themselves at him.

Cash is drinking Patron while getting a lap dance from one of his favorite dancers. Cotton Candy is the one

shaking her high yellow, juicy booty on
him.

CHAPTER 16

At the moment she is hoping that he gets fucked up take her home with him. As he would from time to time. His sex game is just as strong as his money! the X pills he put in her ass is driving her crazy. She is ready to fuck right there even though the club is full of people.

Cash smacking her ass and playing in her pussy. When he spots Jay and Shannon taking a seat with their drinks. Jay sashaying to the song "No Lie" by Drake and Two Chainz. That's her cut she wants to dance for real. Yet she isn't there to party so she plays it cool.

Cash is watching her so hard that his dick grew hard as marble, causing him to dig deeper into Cotton Candy. Her pleasure turns to pain but she doesn't give a fuck right about now.

The hoe is horny enough to let a dog fuck her. Cash begin to look around for one of his flunkies they are all somewhere tricking off.

Cash thinks he is royalty. He doesn't like to move unless it's necessary. At the moment he feels like he couldn't let this bitch get away. Then it came to him as Candy begin to grind harder on his hand.

"Aye Candy do daddy a favor." Cash is telling her more than asking knows that.

"What you need baby?" She looks at him with glassed over eyes, high as hell.

"Do you see that thick chocolate bitch sitting with the slim chick in the red?" He nods at Jay to make sure Candy is following his lead.

"Yeah baby, they cute." She said like a damn fool.

"My thoughts exactly. Go get them tell them I would love for them to join us." He wants to make the bitch feel like she was a part of something other than stripping. She ran off like a trained puppy. That's promised a reward for the task at hand.

She reaches the table tried to smooth her little outfit out hoping she doesn't smell like wet pussy. The two women are laughing and talking to some guys.

The niggas realized she is standing there, the tall dark one said, "What's up Candy?" He is a regular that tricked off in the club hard almost every weekend.

"Hey babe." She is hoping he would not be her plan B tonight. It's nice to know that he is in the building.

"What brings you over here when Cash is in the building?" The tall guy asks. Jealous of the fact that when Cash came to the club hoes acted funny.

"He sent me to ask these beautiful ladies. If they want to join him for a drink in VIP" she stated.

"They good, we chilling over here." This nigga spoke out of turn like someone told him to.

She was about to walk away thinking *"These hoes have bumped their heads to choose them niggas over Cash."* Hell, the name speaks for itself. She is shaking her head when she heard "Hold up little mama, we just met these niggas! They don't speak for us," Shannon told her.

"Oh my bad." She turns back around.

"Yeah who is Cash?" Jay asked as she stand playing her part.

Candy looks her up and down wishing she wasn't coming because she is Cash's type. "He's one of the most important men in this neck of the woods if you know what I mean." She could tell that they aren't from around there with the accent they have.

"Well show us the way to Mr. Important himself." Jay says Shannon follows her. The tall dark guy is pissed as he yelled "Fuck you hoes, thirsty asses." He is tapped on his shoulder by a nigga he doesn't know.

"What up buddy?" He is facing Zane.

"Nigga don't talk to any woman in here like that anymore! If you do I'm gonna blast yo' ass right in the middle of this club." Zane's facial expression is cold as ice. It froze the nigga in his tracks causing him to back away from Zane fall over the table. The crowd erupted with laughter.

Shannon looks over her shoulder giving him a wink that caused him to smile. *"Damn that woman!"*

The three ladies made their way over to Cash. As Jay walks up on him, he begins to sweat. This bitch is ten times badder than he thought she was from afar. Cash is smiling like a hoe at the free clinic.

He is all in. Candy walks over to him tries to wrap her arms around him as she said "Daddy this is Shannon and Jay." She hates Jay even though she doesn't know her.

He pushes her to the side and stepping to Jay but spoke to Shannon first.

"Nice to meet you Shannon. What a beautiful friend you have here." Cash is mesmerized with Jay.

Shannon makes a joke. "That bitch isn't all that." They laughed.

"She all that and then some. Come sit have whatever y'all want, on me" he says to them. Candy went back to her number shaking her ass.

Shannon texts Zane "We going in."

He texts back "Get money!"

Then informs Mack of what's shaking.

CHAPTER 17

Candy still trying her dam nest to get this man's attention. The shit isn't working at all. Shannon sitting there sipping and chopping it up with Cash's right hand man Bang. This nigga is sexy five eleven, shoulder length dreads, slim muscular build all his bottom teeth are dipped in gold.

He has it going on but she isn't about to sleep with the enemy. It's cool to talk with him to pass time though.

Jay is on her job. She moves close to Cash, "Baby tell me, how you got a name like Cash?" she asks like she is clueless.

"Hey baby what can say? I'm made of money" he boasts not knowing he had just signed his death warrant.

"Oh really? Your woman let you come out alone?" Now Jay is leaning in so that her breasts are all his eyes could see.

Candy is shaking her ass hard on the side of his leg it's so funny to Jay. She is irritating the hell out of him. "Aye shorty we had fun tonight. Go on down there work the room get some of that money."

I thought I was going," he cut her ass off fast. Before she could say anything else.

"No baby, go on do yo thang. I'll catch up with you some other time. That's my word." Cash wants her ass to go away from him.

"Promise?" This child is sad it's shameful.

"Scout's honor!" His friends burst out laughing because he always says that when he is lying.

Candy finally takes the walk of shame down to the main floor. Cash feels bad about what he did until Jay says,

"Where were we?" He whips his head back around.

He looks at his watch "I would r love to get to know you better. We can go back to my crib," he says.

"I don't know you like that! You could be crazy or something." She is tickled on the inside as she ran game on the nigga.

"Baby you have my word I will not so much as touch you unless you want me to." Cash staring in her eyes seriously.

Jay looks at Shannon. "I'm not going with you. I'm getting sleepy drinking all this liquor." She is nowhere near drunk with her alcoholic ass.

"Bitch you ain't shit." Jay pretends to fuss.

"You a big girl, you can handle yourself." Shannon lives for the fat jokes.

"I got your big girl hoe," Jay laughs.

"Yes you thick and sexy just the way I love em boo! Please let me spend some time with you outside of here," Cash begs which is something he hasn't done in a while he likes it.

Jay looks at Shannon again than back to him "Ok daddy, let's move." He hops off that seat as if she was going to change her mind. Cash is not about to let that happen.

Shannon sent Zane another text *"We on the move."*

He texts back *"We watching and two steps behind ya'll"*. Shannon smiles at the text.

There is something seriously sexy about her new partner. Maybe she will find out one day. Now just isn't the time.

Cash and his crew escorts the ladies outside. Not watching the niggas that were following close behind them. If Zane wants, he could have domed this nigga right there. That shit isn't going to get him what he is after. So he plays the shit according to plan. Jay and Shannon begin to walk away from the crew. Cash see her going another way.

"Damn boo, that's how you gonna do me?" he asks, hoping not.

"Be easy, I'm walking my girl to her car. Is that cool with you?" Jay asks.

"Aye baby it's yo world, I just want to know you that's all." Cash put his player card up.

"I'll be right back so don't leave me." Jay laughs switching away. Cash watches her with square love in his eyes.

"Never." He meant the words that left his mouth. She just doesn't know how much yet.

The girls walk to the car talking.

"You comfortable with this boo?" Shannon asks her.

"Yeah I'm good, I can handle this. We didn't come this far to throw the towel in now." Jay heart is beating so hard. That she is expecting it to fall out her chest at any moment.

"You know I got to ask "You ready to die?" Shannon hands her the mini three eighty to clip to her bra.

"I'm always ready to die. So much that I will do any and everything to live." Jay heartbeat returns to its normal rate.

"In that case get money!" Shannon hugs her before Jay walks off. She just stands there watching as her friend embraces Cash.

Jay and him got in his car peeling off. Some of the niggas he was with heads home. The others went back in the club for more groupie love. Now that Cash gone they are the cream of the crop.

CHAPTER 18

Zane steps up behind Shannon. "She can handle this. Ya'll been doing this for a long time on ya'll own. We with you now. She got a GPS on her so we know where she at all times." Zane told her.

She looks back at him "How you get the GPS on her?" Shannon wants to know.

"Skull bow clip in her hair. You would never know it's there" he assures her.

"Does she know she got it on her?" She wonders if Jay left her in the dark on this.

"Nope, cause in this game you never know how people gone move or jump ship." Zane know this would piss Shannon off.

She turned to face him. "She would never do that shit!" Shannon is hot.

"I know but we can't take chances." He is trying to help her deal with this. Their boss doesn't play any games or cut any corners.

"What now?" Shannon asks. This is her first out of town mission.

"We wait for her to tell us when to move." Zane see sadness in her eyes. It brought pain to his heart but he doesn't understand why. He wraps his arm around her, "Let's go home boo." He can't believe he said that.

"Home?" Shannon looks at him.

"Girl you know that meant the hotel." He pushes her away from him playfully.

They hopped into the car making their way to the rooms. Mack picked up a honey dip after Jay shook with Cash. The hotel is very quiet as if every soul there is sleeping. They made it to the room where Zane was.

"Are you sleepy?" Shannon asks.

"A little, why?" he need to know.

"I know I'm not gonna sleep much I am wondering if you want to keep me company. We could talk, watch television, whatever just to keep my mind stable." She needs him right now. As much as she hates to admit it he is all she has in this city.

"I don't think I should, its late babe." His mind is telling him to kiss her but he refused to listen to his thoughts.

"Please." She let that slip from her mind out of her mouth.

"Okay, I will. Just never say please again." Shannon is breaking him Zane doesn't like it.

Jay is across town with Cash in the rich folks' neighborhood. It's only a fifteen-minute drive to Irma, South Carolina from the club. The man is definitely getting paper. As they pulled up to his house. Jay thought to herself this nigga lives in a mansion. She can't believe her eyes.

Cash parks his ride hopping out. "Come on mama, this is it." Jay gets out walking very slow. "What's wrong baby?" he asks her.

"You live here alone?" she asks in shock. Her mind is blown.

"Yeah baby, I told you they don't call me Cash for nothing." He is feeling himself. He grabs her by the hand, "Girl come on, you good with me." Jay follows him this time.

They enter the most beautiful place she'd ever seen in her life. The outside has nothing on the inside. He lives at 105 Cedar View Drive. It's a custom built, all brick, four-bedroom home three bathrooms all complete with garden tubs.

The whole third floor is dedicated to a man cave. The living room has a gas fireplace leading into the kitchen which is furnished with top of the line stainless steel appliances. His backyard is stunning with a full patio and outdoor cooking area. Jacuzzi and in-ground pool.

The place is way more than Jay expected. Cash broke her thoughts on the house by handing her a glass of wine.

"So what you think of the place?" Cash loves to wow women with his home.

"I must say you have done very well for yourself." Jay looks around once again.

"It's cool" Cash says, shocked that she isn't acting like a groupie. Little does he know she is it doesn't show on the surface.

"So why did you bring me here? Do you bring all women here?" she asks, assuming he did.

"Because you seem different. Am I right?" He leans close to her.

"Yeah I'm different! There is only one me" Jay says slyly walking over to his sectional.

They talked for what seems like hours. He is a very interesting man. If they had met under different circumstances, she would have loved being his woman but life doesn't always work like that. Some people are born with money, some work hard to get money, but in her case some people take what they want.

The man seems to be clueless to what is happening around him. Cash trusts so easily. That's the worst mistake any hustler could ever make. Just cause the bitch's body is banging and her face was pretty. Doesn't make her less dangerous. In fact, it makes her more dangerous. As usual, men think with their dicks it fucks them over every time.

CHAPTER 19

They ended up falling asleep on the sectional. Jay is awakening by small kisses on the back of her neck. She has to admit they feel very good. She knows that she would have to give up some pussy. Hell, she needs it anyway. Once Cash see isn't going to stop him he asks, "Would you like to go to bed?" He wants to lay her body down do it right.

"Sure baby." He loved the way Jay said that.

Cash room is beautiful. Its cream and gold with a Jacuzzi and steps that lead to a California king bed. The wall has a sixty-inch flat screen television mounted to it. This dude has impeccable taste to be a bachelor.

Jay walks up the steps begins to come out of her clothing. Exposing her nude body as he sits on a gold loveseat that is directly under the television

Cash watches her get comfortable while taking in and loving her body in every way. Healthy women are his biggest weakness.

Jays around on his bed. "Come here daddy! Are you just gonna watch me all night?" she asks.

"I could watch you for the rest of my life." Cash walks over to the bed climbing in. He begins to caress her body as if he is examining a Picasso painting. She moans lightly he loved it. It caused his tongue to take over where his hands left off.

Cash licked her chocolate nipple as if he were licking Godiva chocolate. He licked every inch of her body. Until he reached her cream filled center.

Cash stares at her chocolate center as if it's a masterpiece. She smells sweet he hopes she tasted the same way. The warmth of his breath caused her body to shake a little bit. Cash panting like a dog that hasn't drank in a while. It was beginning to make Jay sick.

She has to say something. "Boy, are you going to eat the pussy or put it on a glass display?" Jay laugh at herself, he joined in with the laughter.

"Oh you got jokes right? Let's see if you'll be laughing after this." Gently he pinches her labia together so that they mimicked lips. He softly kissed those lips just like they are the ones on her face. He could blow a woman's mind with that little trick cause most doesn't understand

that men are born with one mouth.
Women on the other hand have two.

Jay is going crazy from the small kisses. *"Aaarrgghh hummm boy,"* she said looking down at him caressing the top of his head. Cash begins to French kiss that pussy using his tongue and spit causing that thing to get nasty wet.

"Noo hummm uhggg yeess!" Jay screamed. She is cumming but he doesn't care because he has just begun. Cash wants to make sure that every part of her pussy is touched. He used his tongue to trace the letters of the alphabet on that pussy.

Jay's body is shaking so bad that he knows if he doesn't let her go. She would pass out he wouldn't get what he really wants- to feel inside of her.

She is squirming in his arms as holds her. Allowing her get her mind together. Cash know the skills he has so he doesn't give them out often. Especially not to slim women. He only fucked them but they could never be his woman or wife.

Jay begin to kiss his lips. She is sliding her tongue in and out of his mouth. While caressing his rock hard penis. She is ready to feel him inside of

her but she has to taste it first. "Feed me"
she whispered in his ear. Upon hearing
that, he feels like he went blind because
the whole room went black.

When he got his mind right, the
thick goddess has her lips wrapped
around his nine-inch penis sucking it like
a Hoover vacuum on low. Jay grabs his
shaft starts licking all over his penis.

The head is the most sensitive part!
She licks like it was her last meal. She
wants to show him he isn't the only one
with skills! Jays are on point too. Cash is
trying to keep the moans from falling out
of his mouth but they failed him.

"Aye baby, mmm hold on girl." He tries to bark orders.

Jay had his whole member slippery and juicy, making sure her mouth, lips, and face are wet. Pursing her lips tightly together, she slurped his penis into her mouth like a spaghetti noodle while going down his shaft.

Jay sucked on the tip of his penis, sliding her lips up and down him while pressing her tongue on the underside of his penis. Cash has never met a woman that could make him cum giving him head. He doesn't want tonight to be any different.

"Ok shorty I-I-I-I am aggghhh good!" Jay doesn't give a fuck what he talking about. She has a week to make this nigga trust her. She seals the deal when she takes both of his testicles into her wet mouth. Rolling them around on her tongue.

"Ohhh shhhhittt!" he yells as he busts all over her breasts and chin. She watches him shake and tremble then asked, "You ready for this pussy?" Bad as he wanted to he said *"No baby, let's go to sleep.*

"Please!" He grabs her into his arms as if they had been together for years.

She felt some type of way about the

feelings she is feeling for the enemy.

CHAPTER 20

Shannon wakes up on the couch in Zane's arms. She doesn't know what the hell is going on because she was hella drunk when she got back to the hotel. The last thing she remembered is Jay leaving with ole boy Cash.

She pushes Zane startling him causing him to reach for his hip where his gun is. Shannon reaches for the piece she planted on the side of the couch when she first got there.

"Girl what the fuck is wrong with you?" Zane fusses because she caused him to pull a weapon that he knows that he isn't going to use.

"Nigga why are you here holding me and shit?" Shannon has the gun drawn on him as well, but for one reason only, to guard her heart.

"You are one crazy ass bitch! You asked me to stay here with you. Since your home girl went with ole dude." Zane is shaking his head knowing that he should have gone to his own room.

"Boy stop it, I would never..." She has to think about it.

"Yeah shut the fuck up! Your crazy ass did." Zane put the gun away.

Shannon lowers hers as well. She hates this nigga; he thinks he is the shit. She is ready to be done with this lick so she could get away from his ass.

"You shut the fuck up! Get out of my damn room." She opens the door.

"I am glad to leave this muthafucka! Call your girl to see what the progress. So we can be done with this shit." He slammed the door on his way out.

Dallas calling his cell phone as he walked into his room "Yeah!" Shannon has Zane pissed off.

"Wow, what the fuck is wrong with you?" Dallas asked.

"Nothing man, just ready to get this money and be out" Zane huffs.

"The clerk bitch acting up?" Dallas laughs.

"No. Shannon's crazy ass" Zane said.

"Shannon? What has she done?" Dallas know the nigga is sweet on her.

"Man its nothing! She just loopy as hell. It's nothing" he assured him.

"Cool, how we looking right now?" He knows Zane is lying but he doesn't care what the nigga does with his personal life. Dallas is about money.

"Aye Jay on that nigga! She left with him last night. I told Shannon to check in with her before I left her room this morning." Zane assured him shit is going well.

"Left her room this morning?" Dallas laughs. He is the silly type nigga that loves to have fun and joke around.

"Nigga, cut that shit out it's not what you thinking fool." Zane loves Dallas. They have been friends for years. He learned a lot from this man. The main thing is loyalty and love. If he could think of one person, he would hate to lose. It would be Dallas.

"If you say so pimp." He jokes some more.

"Go head on with that shit." Zane had to laugh this time.

"Keep me posted." Dallas throw the boss face back on.

"Yup" Zane says before ending the call.

Shannon has been calling Jay's phone ever since Zane left. She got no answer. She thought a few of the calls were sent to voicemail. She knows that isn't the case so she kept trying to call. After about ten back to back calls she gave it a rest throwing the phone on the couch.

As she paces the floor hoping Jay is okay her phone rings. She snatched it up fast "Jay." She fails to look at the caller ID. Its Jasmine and Nisha on three-way.

"What's hood bitch?" Jasmine chimed.

"Shit." Shannon is glad to hear from them. Disappointed it's not Jay.

"What the hell is wrong with you?" Jasmine says with her big sister hat on.

"Nothing man! Jay left with the nigga we trying to press. Now she's not taking my calls," Shannon states.

"Bitch she good! Jay a big girl trying to get this money. I am down to three bands." Nisha is careless.

"Bitch shut the fuck up! That's on yo' dumb ass." Shannon is pissed. She doesn't like the fact that Jay out there alone.

"Girl don't trip, she gone' call you. It's kind of early you know her ass sleeps late," Jasmine says silently praying for her friend.

"Ya'll stupid. She's good, this is what we do. Remember you're ready to die." Nisha saying that Shannon hangs up. Her mind isn't about to let Nisha's negativity set in.

She begins calling Jay a few more times. It was no use because she didn't pick up. Zane sent Mack to find out what is going on. As him and the clerk bitch went to lunch.

Mack bangs on the door while Shannon is on the other side hoping its Jay. "Finally you came." She opens the door. Mack thinking Zane right, she crazy as hell.

"Zane told you I was coming?" Mack hope she isn't crazy.

"Hell no! Boy bring your crazy ass in here." He looks at her like ain't that the pot calling the kettle black?

"Whatever! What's the word with your girl?" he asked.

"I don't know! I've been trying to reach her. Jay's not picking up," Shannon told him as she walks the floor.

"What? You haven't talked to her? It's four o'clock now! She doesn't know that nigga like that or do she?" Mack is tripping.

"No, she doesn't fucking know him! Jay doesn't move like that!" Shannon fussed. She doesn't know what the fuck to do. All she could do is keep calm and wait for her to answer.

"Well if you trust her like that we just have to wait," Mack says. He trusts his whole squad. So he has to put the new woman on the same page.

"Yeah! Thanks for understanding Mack," Shannon say as she keeps trying Jay's phone.

Mack doesn't know what to do. He doesn't want to tell Zane yet because he would call Dallas. This doesn't look good. Hopefully she will show up soon or at least call. "Aye, babe would you like to go get a bite to eat? Since we're stuck waiting anyway?" he asks.

Shannon looks at thinking "Hell, why not?" She heads out the door without saying a word. Continuing to hit redial on the phone. Mack follows behind her shaking his head. Wondering what kind of trouble these women are gonna bring.

CHAPTER 21

Jay on the other side of town having the time of her life. She knows that she is on a job. Something has changed about the thoughts she had when she came to this city. Verse what she is feeling now.

The man that she is here to set up is sweet, loving, caring, sharing, and fun. Cash is into her begged her to spend the day with him. He has bought her so many things she never had before. There is something about him that says this isn't just for show. It's for real.

Shannon has been blowing her phone up like crazy. Jay knows the crew is looking for her. She just isn't ready to be found yet. The first time she feels something she never had before. Real love.

No man has ever been this nice to her. How could she just throw it all away? Jay doesn't want to rollover on her family either.

She knows that it's time to call Shannon. It's unfair to rollover on her crew they are depending on her to fry the big fish. Jay sitting fancy with Cash as he talks on his phone. After stating it's a call, he had to take.

Cash ignored his phone all day as well. It's been a long time since he found a cool woman. That he likes spending time with. He doesn't know why or where she came from. He is glad she here.

"Baby, I'm going to the ladies' room." Jay taps him as she walks away.

"I'll be right here when you get back baby!" Cash smiles.

"Promise?" She feels like she in high school again. Once she is in the restroom she pulled the phone from her purse. Seeing she had maxed out on text messages, voicemails, and incoming calls.

Jay dials the number hoping Shannon wouldn't answer the phone. Just her luck she picks up on the first ring.

"What?" Shannon is pissed.

"Girl, what's wrong with you?" Jay tries to act as if she doesn't know.

"Bitch really, for real?" Shannon looks at her phone. Wondering if the bitch is smoking dope or something.

"I don't know why you tripping out. I'm here to make the nigga trust me right?" Jay asks.

"Yeah." Shannon has to agree with that.

"One week right?" Jay couldn't believe how well she is lying.

"This is true." Shannon know her girl is doing the team's favor.

"Well, let me work quit blowing me up." Jay playing this shit off so good she shocking herself.

"My nigga! So what we got so far?" Shannon glad she safe more than anything.

"I know the nigga got that bread to blow! Hell he spent ten bands on me already," she boasts.

"Get the fuck out of here bitch! I know you got me something with your greedy ass." Shannon jokes. Her girl pulling this off.

"Bitch I got you. Let me go back to work. We at a fancy restaurant" Jay told her.

"Your lucky bitch! You out living' it up while I'm stuck dealing with these two fools," Shannon complains.

"Who you calling a fool girl?" Mack asks with his face full of food.

"Who is that? Mack's crazy ass?" Jay think he is a cool dude.

"Yeah! He needs to shut up" Shannon fussed.

"You shut yo' ass up." Mack bit his burger.

Jay laughs at them arguing like they had been knowing each other forever.

"Girl, let me get back to setting this nigga up. I'm going to hit you in the morning" Jays says still trying to convince herself.

"You're staying another night?" Shannon is shocked because this not like Jay. This comfortable with a new nigga.

"A week, well six days now right?" Jay putting it on thick.

"Get money boo." Shannon's heart has a funny feeling about this. She has to trust her girl.

Jay ends the call more confused about the situation then she when she first called. She knows that she has to get her mind right. She doesn't know this nigga for real. What Jay don't know is there is a bitch in the bathroom stall listening to her every word

Wondering who it was Jay is laying on. Jay walks out never noticing her as she heads back to her table to finish her meal. She doesn't realize the bitch is tipping behind her to see the nigga she with. The bitch almost dies when she

seen Jay kiss her favorite uncle.

As the duo begin to leave the place.

The young lady calls her uncle's phone.

He picks up on the first ring because it's

his favorite niece. Cash considers her the

daughter he never had.

"Baby, who you love?" Cash asked

her.

"You!" She responds at eighteen.

The same way she did when she was four

years old. Her mother had a drinking

issue her uncle always looked out for her.

The fact that he doesn't have children

don't hurt either.

"What you need babe?" Cash forever buying her shit she is spoiled.

"Nothing. I need to talk to you in person." She never talked this way it caught him off guard.

"You good or you need me to come now?" Cash asks not wanting to end what he is doing.

"No, meet me tomorrow" she says.

"Cool." He glad because he wants to spend as much time with Jay as he could.

Cash on cloud nine he doesn't know what it was about this woman. That has him so open. She is sexy as hell the black

Vera Wang dress he got for her is blessing her body right now.

If he has things his way, he plans to make her his main woman. Cash hasn't felt this way in years. He loving every moment of it. Nothing is going to stand in his way of making this a permanent feeling.

CHAPTER 22

Shannon and Mack made it back to the hotel. They are laughing and talking shit. About how Jay had the nigga coming out of his pocket for her.

"That nigga a sucker tricking off on a bitch. He just met last night in a strip club." Mack dying laughing.

"Hey, what can I say. My nigga got that STL swag!" Shannon proud of her girl.

"High five on that because I got these country hoes wilding out here." Mack pops his collar.

"Fool, get yo' bitch ass on." Shannon jokes with him.

"Watch your mouth girl." Mack pushes her. It's something about her that make him feel like a big brother. He likes it because all his family dead.

They when on a family outing. While he was at his aunt's house sick with the chicken pox. When they died in a six car pile-up caused by a high speed chase.

Mack's aunt kept him for the money. The city paid for the loss of his mother, father, sister, and baby brother. She ran through that money fast. Stunting with all her friends in a five-year time span she fucked up a million dollars. Mack was

fourteen by this time. His aunt was

depressed and strung out on dope from

fucking up that money.

As soon as he found a way to move

out. He left never looking back.

They are laughing and slap boxing
in the lobby heading to the elevators.
They didn't see Zane at the counter until
he yells "Aye, where ya'll been?" he asks
as if he their daddy.

"Nigga, none of your damn business!
Did we ask where you and the clerk
went?" Shannon can't stand him going on
a date with that rude bitch.

"Hater." Zane smiles.

"Whatever!" Shannon isn't hating! That bitch ugly.

Zane was about to say something when Mack cut him off. Informing him what has taken place. Zane glad to hear things are going smooth being he thought the game had changed.

They took the elevator up to their rooms. Shannon unlocks her door when Mack says "Sis, lunch tomorrow on me." He enjoys her company.

"I wouldn't miss it big bruh" Shannon says closing her door.

Zane looks at both of them real strange follows Mack in the room calling Dallas.

Zane rapped on the phone with Dallas schooling him on how shit is shaping up. Dallas happy to hear that things are going according to plan. He hates when shit off track cause when there is no order, muthafuckas can lose their lives fast.

Dallas taught his team to follow orders because one faulty move could cost you your life.

Dallas don't give a fuck who it is. If they moved funny style on the squad. It's an order to put their ass down right then and there. He isn't into torturing niggas. He lives by the ride or die code. If he finds out you're not a rider. Dallas domes you right then and there for the world to see. His crew isn't to be fucked with.

Dallas family is one you could never leave. Once you were in the only way out is death. He has to do it this way because letting a muthafucka walk. Means you allowing them to talk. Talking leads to indictments, life sentences, and death in numbers. To avoid that issue you ride or die for the Duffle Bag Crew.

Zane got off the call glad to share the news with his boss. Mack has been on his phone caking with some bitch. Then he jumped off the phone. "Bruh, how the boss holding up?" he asks as he grabs his jacket to leave.

"He good now that we going to be bringing this paper in real soon." Zane spoke like he has an issue with Mack.

"Your cool nigga?" Mack picks up on hoe shit a mile away.

"Yeah! man I'm good" Zane says raising his voice.

"Aye, nigga what the fuck is up with that shit?" Mack pissed.

"Man nothing! Go where you going."
Zane waved him off.

Mack is about to chew his ass out.
When he thinking about this lil' light skin
thick booty bitch. That's waiting for him
to dick her down. He heads for the door
thinking she gone suck all the stress out
of me. Mack hand on the knob.

"Why you ask her to lunch nigga?"
Zane hates what he feeling for a woman
he never even kissed.

Mack chuckles because he knows
this is what the shit about. He has to
admit he is shocked. Zane known for

fucking hoes passing them right along to the next nigga.

"Shannon is cool man. She reminds me of my sister I lost. I just like her company." Mack looks at his confused friend. Who is hurting because he had just questioned his dude over a bitch.

"That's what's up nigga. I'm out of order that's isn't my bitch to be questioning your fam. Enjoy your night my dude." Zane checked his self.

"Look fam, I know you nigga! I am watching you peep lil' mama. Why not step to her? Dallas isn't fucked up about us dating within the crew as long as it doesn't affect business." Mack wants to see his dude happy. At least once in this life.

Zane has everything a nigga wants but never had love.

"Man you know that square shit ain't for me. Even if I want to do it. I would fuck it up some way." Zane needs to clear his mind. He has to stop thinking about this woman.

"Well nigga you know best. Don't sweat it if you not gonna act on it." Mack hit the door never hearing him say *"I'm scared of love."* Zane glad no one heard the words that left his mouth.

CHAPTER 23

Cash has Jay at his crib again for another night he elated. He could tell he has this woman's full attention. Jay don't have his. His mind wondering what his niece wants to talk to him about. Jay sees the tension on his face asking,

"What's the matter daddy?" Jay really cares.

"It ain't shit baby." Cash grabs her placing her in his lap.

Jay looks into his eyes for the first time. She realizes they are hazel gray. Jay wants to know his story. What he really about? She hopes something he says causes her to do the job she came to do. Right now she in love with the enemy.

Cash looks at her "What you thinking shorty?" He asks.

"Shit" Jay lies.

"Yes you are! So speak on it," he demands.

"I want to know who you really are Cash." Jay looks away from him.

"I'm Cash baby." He put his swag on.

Jay looks at him like he playing games. She stupidly about to fuck over her crew for a nigga. Whose government she doesn't know.

"I am Sincere Williams; I am the nigga that many don't like because I'm getting money. I have been hustling since my tenth birthday. My ole man was a hustler that got killed right before my eyes.

The nigga could have domed me too he didn't. Told me if I feel some type of way about what he done to get at him when I am grown. I grew up about a month later took over the hood.

Niggas don't like that shit. They respect it got down with the cause. I don't love hoes. I fuck them the only people I bring here are bitches. That's me boo."

Cash feels weird talking to this woman as if he known her forever.

'Sincere, I like that name." Jay smiles.

"Really? I hate it. People think I'm soft when they hear my name. I started going by Cash. Only a few people know my real name so feel special lady." He smiles at her.

"I do feel special; I think it's time for me to go back to my world. Before I get too comfortable." Jay is honest for the first time.

"Can I trust you?" he asks her.

"With your life." Jay cold blooded for that shit.

Cash taps on her ass "Stand up shorty!" She moves he get begins to walk down this long ass hallway. Cash opens the door his hand the key.

The door came open by sliding it back into the wall. He enters the room.

"Are you coming?" Jay scared as hell. Not knowing what the room holds.

"Yeah." Jay walks in she thought she would pass the fuck out. Each wall made of money that's held in place by glass. She never seen anything like this in her life.

Jay can't find words.

Cash know that he has blown her mind. "What were you saying about getting comfortable?" he asked.

"I am saying this isn't my life. I should go." Jay is getting light head surrounded by so much fucking money.

"You can be comfortable here whenever you like shorty." Cash dead ass serious.

"You don't even know me like that." Jay tries to ignore what he saying.

"You don't know me either! However, you've been here for two days. If I want to kill you I could have. Your people

wouldn't have known where you were."
Cash schools her ass real fast.

"Why did you show me this shit dude?" Jay confused as fuck. Those racks about to make her come. She starts to walk out of the room. He jumps in front of the door once she on the other side.

"I want you baby, for real! I can give you everything you want and never had." Cash holding her now.

"Let go! Why would you do that for a woman that you don't know?" Jay knows it's time to shake this. It's too much for her.

"To show you I'm for real about all the shit I am saying. If you want to go I will let you." Cash not going to beg.

"I want to go to bed," Jay says.

"So you want to give this thang a try for real?" Cash feels like a kid in a candy store.

"Yeah baby, let's do it." Jay don't know what she going to tell her crew. To keep the off this man. She will have to do something. Jay isn't about to let this meal ticket she in the palm of her hands go. Not this time.

She thought back long ago. When she first got down with her team. *A man*

238 | P a g e

she loved dearly was moving major weight. He was a great man when it came down to providing for her. He never fully loved her the way she needed to be loved.

When her crew decided to make him a target she was down with it. The love she had for him is what caused her to be okay with killing him. No matter how much she confessed her love, it didn't move him.

He would always tell her that words have no meaning. When he would talk to her about his children and baby's mother. She realized where the love she been seeking was.

Jay always asked that he keep it real with her. He never did, and even when she was hurting it didn't seem to matter much to him. When the time came to take him out she never even hesitated. In her heart he was already dead.

Now she was with a man that was promising her everything she had been asking for and she wasn't about to miss out on that. She would face the music when the time came, but for now she would enjoy the moment.

CHAPTER 24

Three weeks later...

Dallas pissed with the crew because they haven't made the move he needs to be made. Most of all Jay M.I.A. shit is fucked up.

Shannon in a bad place because the last time she spoke to Jay she was right on track. They don't know what is going on with her. Her number has been changed, no one half heard nor seen her. Not even her mother that's her style.

Dallas called a group meeting because shit needs to change drastically. Everyone was in attendance at the meeting: Zane, Shannon, Mack, Nisha, Jasmine, and Dizzy. Dizzy waiting in the wings along with Jasmine and Nisha. The call never came then crew the out in the field came home. Truth be told, Dizzy never went out to lay on a muthafucka because he isn't built that way.

He isn't a ladies' man rather subdued, only coming to life during sex and when it's time to kill. Dallas always keep him in the cut until he is needed.

Dallas walks around the office warehouse looking dapper as always. He had a meeting with his hoes earlier that day to see where their heads were. If they were still loyal. These aren't average street walkers. These hoes wear red bottoms on their feet, diamonds graced their necks and wrists, they drive expensive cars, and lives in a luxurious home.

Outside looking in you would have never guess how these women make their money. To maintain their lifestyle, they must remain loyal to Dallas.

Now he meeting with the Duffle Bag Crew. They were in some deep shit.

"Family." Dallas always greets them that way at important meetings.

"United," they chimed in. It's the crew's mission statement. To them the word hold so much weight there is no need to say any more.

"We have a target that we can't seem to touch. Is this true?" Dallas scans the room to see who would speak up.

"No one is untouchable," Zane spoke.

"Well, why are we here talking instead of counting money?" Dallas walks over to his chair.

"We have a traitor in the squad," Mack states.

Shannon's eyes bulged out of her head thinking how dare he. The thought was broken by Dallas saying "I think we do."

"What the fuck you trying to say?" Shannon pissed.

"Who the hell you talking to girl?" Dallas steps close to her. Zane's body movement told Dallas he doesn't like that.

"You!" Shannon stares him in the eyes. Mack and Zane smiles. This why both men loved her so much. Never bows down to anyone, not even Dallas.

"What the fuck I say? Your girl is M.I.A. she the person luring in the target. Now she disappears into thin air?" Dallas loves Shannon's G code. He smiling on the inside, he doesn't let it meet the surface.

"How the fuck do you know she isn't dead?" Shannon heated now.

"If she isn't, she will be." Dallas so serious.

This caused Jasmine to chime in. "What the fuck you mean she will be?" she asks.

"Jay has violated this family no one gets away with that." He looks at her to make sure she comprehends what is said.

"This is some bullshit!" Jasmine not about talking about killing her bestie.

"It's her own fault, she probably got greedy said fuck us." Nisha jumps in.

"Bitch fuck you! This shit yo' fault. If you hadn't fucked up your money. We would have been good for a while." Jasmine can't believe this bitch.

"You called me first, this is true Jasmine, no matter how good you are when money is in the field. You go get it," Dallas schools her.

"I'm out this bitch." Jasmines to the door to leave looking back to see if Shannon and Nisha are coming with her neither one budged. This made her look at them in a different light.

Jasmine pulls the door open Dallas says "You can leave this meeting if it's too personal for you! You can't leave this family alive." Jasmine let the door slam on his words.

Shannon just as pissed as Jasmine. She can't leave Jay to the wolves. Nisha don't give a fuck, she about the money. She with whatever it takes to get what she wants. That is the only reason she signed up for this bullshit. Nobody is going to stand in her way.

Shannon asks, "Dallas send me back let me find her. Give me a week. Better yet I will find her and that nigga. One week please? If I don't fix this. Then shit is out of my hands We move on to the new target in N.Y."

CHAPTER 25

Dallas know all he needs to know about the nigga in N.Y. He can get him at any time he isn't planning to put a bitch on him. The nigga a homo thug will have Zane befriend the nigga. Then lay him down take his money. The nigga a major stunner. He run his mouth too much let every muthafucka know where he lays his head. The nigga is an easy target.

Dallas know allowing Shannon a week she asking for isn't an issue. Plus, he knows her G-code. If he doesn't give it to her she damn sure to take it anyway.

"If I grant you this week to look for your friend. What will you do when you find her?" Dallas is curious.

"If she on bullshit, she's as good as dead." Shannon isn't bullshit. She pissed with Jay right now. Shannon wants to hear her out even if she does have to air her ass out.

Mack and Zane's head whips in her direction because they couldn't believe their ears. Its wild how money can fuck up a friendship. Dallas likes Shannon's answer. He needs to know why she willing to rollover on her friend like that.

"Why?" Dallas asked her hoping that he don't have to kill her ass where she stands.

"If she chose a nigga over me leaving me for dead. She's already dead to me." Shannon dead ass serious. She hurt in her heart by this shit Jay pulled. She wants to believe that the nigga kidnapped her friend. Holding her hostage, but she knows that isn't the case this time around.

Dallas was good with the answer she gave; he feels the same way.

"Cool! You have your week. Only a week nothing more. After that I am going

to find them and their both dead. Deal?"
He stretches his hand for them to shake
on it.

Shannon lit a cigarette looking at
his hand "Deal!" She never shook it. She
walks out with Nisha in tow. Dallas has
to laugh at the woman after his own
heart. She all woman but she moves like
a man. That turns Dallas on in so many
ways. He thought about the women in his
crew. How they move; Shannon in a
league of her own!

Zane and Mack watches her leave,
loving her strength. Dallas broke their
thoughts. "Mack I want you to go back to

South Carolina with Shannon." Dallas spoke to him like his mind somewhere else.

"Zane." Dallas is cut off by Zane "I know you want me to go befriend this ole fruit bag ass nigga. I'm telling you now that I'm going in like I'm looking for a N.Y. connection. Not any homo shit if dude flip before he shows me his crib.

I swear you won't see a dime of that nigga money because I will kill him on the spot!" Zane leaves the warehouse.

Mack and Dallas watches him walk out. Dallas throw his hands up in the air, "What the fuck is this? Get pissed and walk out on Dallas day? I'm just trying to get money without killing a muthafucka from my own crew. Damn is that too much to ask for?"

"Yup." Mack know Dallas a good dude that's tries to look out for everyone in his crew. "Dallas man, they're not mad at you. Shit off track with the girls. They've always been down for each other. Right now Jay got shit looking real fucking suspect." Mack tries to comfort his home boy.

Dallas looks at him trying to take his words in, then asking, "Zane, why he tripping?" He shakes his head.

"You know he hate bitches! You always sending his cute ass out when niggas on that funny style shit. Plus, he in love." Mack laughs because he was feeling Zane's pain.

"I know he is, that's why I sent you with Shannon instead of him because I don't want love to get him or her killed." Dallas went to the back of the warehouse that led to his home. He needs a drink.

Mack let himself out. He has to go get Shannon so they could catch the red eye as soon as possible.

CHAPTER 26

Jasmine over this shit She looking for a way out. She isn't sure how she is going to make this shit happen. Dallas made it known from day one. That you can't leave this family no matter what. She never thought she want to leave. Shit has changed so much in such a small amount of time. Jasmine doesn't know what the fuck to do.

She holding a nice piece of change. It's far from enough to relocate her family to a place where Dallas couldn't find her. Jasmine in her box smoking Kush blunt as if it's some reggie.

She tripping hard her thoughts are broken by the phone ringing. "Who the fuck is this?"

She hates numbers she doesn't know. Not to mention feeling some type of way due to the way shit going on right now. Jasmine trust is at an all-time low.

"It's me sis," Jay says.

Jasmine's mind is blown. This hoe calling like she hasn't been missing for almost a month. The most fucked up part is she calling like she good. When Jasmine would have bet her life that the nigga done some foul shit to her home girl.

She isn't trying to hear that shit. Dallas talking about saying she rolled over on her crew! It seems like he is on to something.

"J-J-Jay is that you?" Jasmine stutters because her brain is scrambled at the moment.

"Yeah bitch, what's good fam?" Jay talks like shit still on track and nothing is wrong.

"Jay, are you high on something more than weed ma?" Jasmine ask It's the only muthafuckin' way that someone's mind could be this fucked up.

"Bitch, no!" She has nervous laugh like she knows shit isn't cool.

This shit pissed Jasmine off to the highest level. "Bitch, are you out of your fucking mind? Calling me like there isn't a fuckin price on your head?" she asks.

"Price on my head? What the fuck you mean?" Jay has lost her mind from the great sex and shopping sprees she been indulging in.

"Yes a fuckin' price! What the fuck you think this is? A muthafuckin' game! You could have fucked over me, Shannon, and Nisha. If this was our own lick.

We with Dallas' team now! It's blood in blood out. I guess you planning to pay with our fuckin' lives!" Jasmine is hurting in her soul.

"Jazz I'm sorry, you don't understand. I was going to go along with the plan. I just couldn't once I got to know Cash. He's a great man that gives me the world. He loves me for real. Cash wants to get married have a baby.

I know I should have kept it real with ya'll. So ya'll could move on to the next target. What do you want from me? I'm in love" she pleads her case.

Jasmine's mind is spinning. *"In love? A good dude? Marriage? Children?"* This hoe done bumped her head somewhere. She can't be this heartless, or could she?

"Jasmine, you understand right? You have a husband and children." She knows that Jasmine's family is her soft spot. Jay trying to get back in her good graces.

"First thing, bitch don't use my family to win me over. Secondly, you a trifling, low class, no counting, sorry ass desperate bitch that chose dick over family! That's sorry. I know that you are sorry.

Lastly, don't ever call me again cause you dead to me. Once Dallas reaches you and that nigga! Neither of you will be able to ever blow a spit bubble again! So I guess you can count breathing out as well." Jasmine slams the damn phone down so hard it shatters.

She so hot you would think she invented hell. Jasmine know what she needs to do. She has to contact Dallas to let him know that she is sorry. He was right about Jay. She needs to inform him the game has changed.

It's time for the team to fuck this issue with no grease. So they could move on with their lives.

Jay is hurt in her own way even though she has no room to be. She assumed Jasmine would have her back on this no matter what. Now that isn't the case, she feels the crew doesn't love her. They just wanted to use her as bait.

She knows if they could see the man she sees. They would let it all go. Jay doesn't know what she is going to do. This time she is choosing herself and love first.

Cash is gone to meet his niece, she is finally able to take a long bath and clear her mind. Jay hopes one day her friends will understand that her heart got in the way.

Little does she know, after Dallas loss Keisha he has a soft spot for love. If she had stepped to him correctly, he would have taken her views into consideration. Sometimes real love forms in the strangest place. He would've never stood in the way of that.

Dallas favorite saying is *"It's not what you do, it's how you do it."* At this point Jay was out of order.

CHAPTER 27

Cash pushing a white V8 Vantage Roadster white leather. He a dope boy that floss the way he makes his money by pushing a white on white. No matter what type of ride it is, all his cars are that way.

He has been blowing his niece off for a few weeks now. Cash doesn't mean to he just couldn't help it. Jay putting that pussy down on him like she serving crack. She his pusher he is hooked.

Its mind blowing to him that he had just met this woman. Cash has fallen head over heels in love with her. He knows that its possible. Hell he had seen niggas walk away from their wife and kids for a certain kind of bitch.

Cash thought it would never happen to him. He thought those niggas were suckers to fall for a bitch that fast.

Now here he is allowing a bitch to shop as much as she wants. His other hoes are mad as shit. Yet not enough to stop waiting until he finds a way to fit their dumb asses in. Jay the sweetest woman he has ever met.

She cooks, cleans, and the sex is mind boggling. The thought of fucking that bitch makes him bust in his pants. The way she fucking and sucking this man should be illegal. There isn't going to be shit that stands in the way of keeping her around.

He pulls up to his mom's house where his niece is waiting for him. She didn't allow him to park before she jumps in the car. "Let's ride!" She has a serious look on her pretty face. Cash pulled off hitting the highway so they could ride.

"Unc', how have you been?" she asks. As if he living with some terminal ill disease. She waiting for him to die from soon.

"I'm great actually this is the happiest I've been in years." Cash smiles at her wondering what is on her mind.

"What's got you so happy?" She hopes he isn't still seeing the same woman she overheard in the bathroom.

Cash begin to smile as he thinks about Jay. "I think I found the one Mariah." He cheesing hard.

"Who is she Cash?" Mariah asks. The fact she called him Cash made his stomach turn. It's something about the way she said it.

"What did you call me Mariah?" Cash pissed because of the way it made him feel.

"I mean who is she Unc'?" she asks rephrasing her question.

"Jay, her name is Jay shed moved here from the STL. Looking to start her life over, she ran into a nigga like me at the club. I jumped down on her now she's mine. I never felt this way about a woman Mariah." Cash in a daze as he talked.

"Well, what about me?" Mariah somewhat jealous and pissed this woman has him open but here to set him up.

"Mariah you know you are my number one queen. I will tell you this, get ready to share me with queen number two I'm gonna ask her to marry me." She couldn't believe her ears.

"Marry her? You don't fucking know this hoe!" She thinking, *"Damn them STL bitch's pussy must be made of gold."*

"Why the hell are you cursing? Calling her out of her name Mariah? You haven't met her! Once you do, you will love her just as I do." He sounds sure about the shit that spilled from his mouth.

He looks at his Rolex like he has some where to be then at Mariah. "What is it you wanted to talk to me about girl?" She doesn't know what to say.

She wants to tell him about the bathroom call she overheard. Mariah can't bring herself to break his heart. She knows bitches use him for his money.

Now he feels like he found love. Who is she to take that from him? She can't do that to him. She plans to bring it to this bitch as soon as possible.

Mariah doesn't know what to tell him. Now that he happy and shit she throw herself under the bus. "I'm pregnant!" She is the nigga responsible isn't an upstanding guy.

Now that she is knocked up he playing her shady talking out the side of his neck. Saying the child isn't his truth of the matter, it might not be.

Cash is speechless. He doesn't want to think about her fucking. Damn sure not having a baby. He doesn't have babies yet he is hurt. "Why ma?" He taught her how to be safe. He knows he couldn't stop her.

"He said he loved me! That he would always be there for me." She feels better now that she talking to someone about it.

"I guess he don't now, right?" Cash slowly dying inside trying to hold his tears in.

"No, he doesn't!" She begins to cry. "That's why you have to be careful who you let in your life" she sniffled.

"I will be careful don't worry about me. I'm always one step ahead of the game." She thinking *"Not this time you sleeping with the devil."*

Mariah is getting sleepy. "Unc can you take me back to Big Ma's house?" She needs to rest.

"Sure love, we not done with this baby thing. What are your plans?" Cash needs to know where she stands on the issue.

"I am having this baby Unc. No man gone make me murder a child that didn't ask to be here." She is pissed now.

"Whoa, slow your tone down shorty. I ain't put that baby in there. You feel me?" She hates when he talks.

"I know this." She is ready to get out the car. Big Ma's house a few blocks away.

"Understand this baby nor you will want for anything." She whips her head toward him. As Cash pulls in the drive way. She never understood why this man so good to her. Of course she is his sister's daughter. She isn't about shit. She wants to ask him so what better time than now.

"Why do you love me so much? I know I'm your niece. However, you love me no matter what I do. Right or wrong." Mariah needs to know before she exits the car.

Cash stares out the driver's side window for a while. He could remember the day like it was yesterday.

"A few months before you were born. Me, yo' daddy, and our home boy Pop was kicking it on that corner right there. Your

daddy and I jammed up a nigga spot a

few weeks before. We were chopping it up

and smoking loud. When a black Chevy

with tinted windows rolled up on us real

slow. When the nigga upped that thang,

we all took off running. I thought we were

good until I realized Bebop, your daddy,

wasn't behind me.

As I ran back to the corner a nigga

was out the whip dumping a round into

his body. I reached for my heat domed the

nigga. His crew peeled off after they saw

the nigga head explode." Cash stops

talking he doesn't want to go on.

"What happened next?" Mariah needs this closure. She has tried to get the whole story out of her mom for years.

"I walked up to Bebop he was still moving. I heard the police closing in a few miles away. I didn't know what to do or say. I was looking in the dying eyes of my best friend and brother-in-law.

He said 'Leave me here I'm already dead'." I am trying to tell him no, but with the little energy he had he pushed me off him. So hard blood began to spill from his mouth and nose even with that he managed to say,

"Go. Someone has to take care of my daughter." I looked at him with tears falling from my eyes. He held up his fist for a pound to know my word was bond. Once our fist connected the life left his body. I took off running from the crime scene."

Mariah cries her heart out by the end of the story. Cash is too, but he does it for her. She needs to know the truth; her dad was a great man. That wants nothing but the best for her. Cash gave her just that.

She gets out of the car feeling brand new. Mariah know that she needed to get close to Jay. She isn't about to lose her uncle, too.

"Hey can you come get me tomorrow to crash at your crib? I don't get much rest here." She lies.

"Sure thing boo. You can meet my lady and ya'll can go find you a nice place of your own out there by me!" She was shocked and excited to be getting her own crib.

"I love you Cash," she chuckled.

"All the ladies do." She watched the only man she really loved drive away and knew that she had to do whatever it took to keep him around.

CHAPTER 28

Dallas hold the phone listening to Jasmine run the dime down. He was hoping he was wrong. "Jasmine I'm sorry. I wanted to be wrong." He tells her.

"I wanted you to be wrong, too." She says with sadness in her heart.

"I know this is going to be hard for you. The crew has to lay them down and take the money like we planned." Dallas know she understands that Jay good as dead, too.

"It's not going be hard to kill someone that's already dead to me. Call me when it's time to move." She hangs

up. Dallas loves the gangster in these
women.

"Hello!" Zane chimes. He in good mood today. He has go to New York to link up with this homo thug. She decides to get him three of the baddest bitches his city has to offer last night for a night of fucking. Oh yes, they did the damn thing. This nigga feeling himself this morning Dallas know it.

"Look who's turnt up in this muthafucka today!" He laughs at his partner. Zane the dog out of the whole pack, hands down.

"Yeah you know how a G do. Just sent three bad bitches home. If I was square they would've had a nigga open ya dig," he boasts, loving his life to the fullest.

"I dig, but every bitch ain't Shannon." Dallas a nigga that loves to put fire under a muthafucka's feet.

"There you go with that bullshit. Nigga look, get the fuck off my phone with that lame ass shit." Zane is pissed again.

"Damn that's how you talk to ya boss?" He fucking with him now.

"Nigga you ain't my boss, we fam. What the hell you want anyway? I got to lay on this hoe ass nigga you got me fucking with." Zane hates bitch niggas.

Dallas always putting him on their ass because he a pretty nigga that has a monster living inside of him.

"There's been a change of plans." Dallas has a different tone of voice now.

"What we got to do?" Zane wants to know so he could make it happen.

"Jay called Jasmine on some next dimension shit. As if she has no clue that she fucked up in a major way," he informs Zane.

"Really? She said fuck the crew for real?" Zane had a funny feeling about bringing these hoes on anyway, this is why: Dick and money can blindside a hoe causing her to rollover on her mama. Never mind her crew.

"What's the next move?" Zane asks.

"Find them, take the money, and kill them it's simple." Dallas puffs his Cuban.

"You coming out to work?" Zane quizzed him.

"Do I need too?" he asks knowing that answer.

"Not at all, this is for baby piranhas not sharks ya dig." Zane says because Dallas put so much work down in his life! It's funny he still alive.

"Go eat the goldfish." Dallas ends the call.

Mack and Shannon has made it to South Carolina. They got the call shortly after arriving there. Shannon hasn't said much since they arrived. They are posted at the club where Jay linked up with Cash the first time. They spotted them then followed them home.

The two look like love birds. Shannon livid by the whole scene. She wants to murk Jay the first moment she saw her with Cash. Dallas gave direct orders to only follow her movement.

Mack and Shannon has been doing this for the past three days. They watched his house, her shopping with a young lady they think his daughter. Then turns out to be his niece. The two ate lunch and shopped for baby items. This made Shannon wonder if Jay is expecting. The shit phony, it just doesn't seem real. That her girl made such a decision.

The young girl with her has an ulterior motive for befriending Jay. Shannon know Jay, she doesn't mix well with many people. It's impossible she made this man's family embrace her that fast.

This shit is making Shannon sick to her stomach. They decide to fall back this

Thursday night, plus Zane, Nisha, Jasmine, and Dizzy are coming into town. Dizzy stays in the cut because he insane. This nigga serious with the artillery. He doesn't bullshit when it's time to go to war.

The nigga six foot five, one hundred and fifty pounds, light skinned with green-gray eyes and diamonds in each ear. His swag on a thousand. The boy looks like a gangster version of the singer Prince. He isn't to be fuck with.

The knock on the room door is expected. Mack is in Shannon's room. He opens the door facing his crew. Zane smiles at him, and grabbing him in for a hug.

"Man if ya'll don't move the fuck out my way with that gay ass shit, I'm gonna pop both ya'll ass." Jasmine and Nisha is shocked at the way Dizzy talking. The nigga was silent the whole damn flight.

"Oh you got vocal capability now?" Nisha says.

Jasmine chimes in, "It's alive!" They all laughing, always playing too much.

"Aye you hoe don't know me. I will fuck you bitches up" he barks at them.

The three of them stands there yelling and arguing. Mack dying laughing at Jasmine trying to hit Dizzy but Nisha

holding her back.

CHAPTER 29

Dizzy keeps saying "You got me fucked up." The funny thing about Dizzy, as crazy as he is he would never hit a woman. Even if she hit him, he would just curse her the hell out.

The shit doesn't make no sense. It seems like a room full of siblings, not a certified squad. Shannon had even she yells,

"Everybody shut the fuck up!" Her mind all over the place Shannon isn't about to let them drive her crazy.

"Who the fuck she thinks she is?" Dizzy asks eyeballing her.

"Look you behind the wall bitch ass nigga, I'm Shannon! That's the first thing you need to know. Secondly I'm not to be fucked with, ever!" She closes to him looking up in his face.

He looks down at her saying, "You make my dick hard talking to me like that." She smiles backing away from him.

Zane about to pass the fuck out. He needs some air. "Fellas let's head to our room. We have some planning to do. So that we are prepared for tomorrow. You ladies should get some rest too." The three men exits the.

Jasmine shakes her head as they left. Nisha of course ready to hit the ground running. Dallas told them to lay low because shit going to take place Saturday. They have no more time to waste. "Where are you going?" Shannon asks Nisha.

"Bitch I'm going out! I know Cash ain't the only one balling out here." She priming her little slim body. As if it looks good in the sleek black mini dress.

"Dallas said to stay in tonight and Friday night because Saturday we move." Shannon big on the orders set in place because their design to keep them safe.

"Fuck Dallas, he doesn't own me! I'm not a hoe he got on the strip." She walks out the door.

"He owns us all," Shannon says shaking her head at a closed door.

Jasmine don't give a fuck, "That's on that bitch! Who's about to go to bed is me." Shannon laughs at her sister knowing that this all will be over soon. She ready to get back to her daughter.

CHAPTER 30

Jay on the other side of town, playing house with her nigga. Cash stepped out while Mariah in the guestroom sleeping. The smell of fried chicken, smothered potatoes, sweet corn, collard greens and golden honey cornbread awakened her.

She heads straight towards the kitchen. "Wow it smells amazing in here!" Mariah chimes, she and the baby are hungry.

"You ready to eat, ma?" Jay asks like a regular ole Suzy homemaker.

"Yeah aunty." Mariah has been calling her this for a few weeks now. She is used to it Jay fixed a plate handing it to her. The child eats like she hasn't eaten in months. Babies will do that to you.

"Girl slow the hell down if you choke and die! Your uncle gonna kill me," Jay jokes.

The word kill made Mariah think of the phone call she heard Jay having a few months ago. The woman she looking at now isn't the same woman she overheard.

This woman loves her uncle. She knows the day she gets to confront Jay would come. What better time than now? Mariah moving to her new place in a few days on with her on life she goes.

Jay washing dishes humming when Mariah says, "Can I ask you something?" Jay wants to say no.

"Sure baby girl, what's good?" Jay's heart beating like the bass drum on the drum line.

"Why did you come here from St. Louis?" Jay told Cash her real home town.

"To change my life for the better." Jay praying, she buys that lie.

"The phone conversation you had at the restaurant a month ago. Is that the way you plan to better your life?" Mariah stopped eating now staring her down hoping she doesn't continue to lie.

Mariah grown to love Jay she understands why her uncle crazy about this woman. She treats him like a king on the throne. Cash never has to ask her to do anything. If he does, it's never asked twice!

"Mariah, I..." Jay can't believe she was in the bathroom with her. When she made the call to Shannon.

"Jay please tell me the truth. I never told my uncle, When I wanted to he displayed so much love for you. That I couldn't bring myself to tell him.

I know why he loves you, because I do too! It won't stop me from killing you right now. Then explain why I had to do it." She places the 40 glock she has on the table for Jay to see she's not bullshitting.

"Ok Mariah. I can tell you why I'm here, but not who I work for," Mariah raises her eyebrows Jay continues, "Use to work for." She rephrases the statement.

"Tell me everything." Something tells Jay this was a life or death situation. She better speaks now or forever hold her peace.

"I'm with the Duffle Bag Bitches. That may not hold much weight here but in the Lou that name mean that you're looking for trouble." She informs the young lady.

"So what do you do?" Mariah is intrigued by Jay's title.

"We set hustlers up, taking what they have all of it when possible." She feels like shit telling the niece of the man she is supposed to set up.

"The conversation I overheard is why you're here, am I correct?" Mariah had turned in to a baby boss. She loving every minute of it too.

"Yes!" Jay lowers her head.

"I should kill you right now, right?" Mariah trying to feel her out.

"If that's what you see fit to do ma." Mariah loves her heart.

"I want to see my uncle happy. Can you do that?" she asks.

"Yes Mariah! I can do that." Jay is telling the truth; she has truly fallen in love with Cash.

"Really?" She drags the shit out to see what Jay would say.

"Mariah, I am not gonna beg you for my life. When my crew tracks me down. I'm as good as dead any fucking way. I fucked over the only people that ever gave a fuck about me." Jay getting pissed off now.

"Why?" Mariah needs to know. What would make someone do that? Especially for someone they barely know.

"I came here with every intention to take your uncle down. Once I got to know him, I fell for him. I can't tell you why. I got a crew of people mad, hurt, and disappointed with me. I can live with that if it means spending the rest of my life with Cash. That's my word. I can't make you believe me; all I can do is show you. If you give me the opportunity." At this point Jay done explaining herself Mariah knows it.

"One thing I need you to do," Mariah says. She wants them to be together. However, if Cash ever finds out she lied to him, he gone lose it.

"You have to tell him the truth. He hates a liar." Mariah schools her on the man she loves.

"I can't, he will hate me or kill me!" Jay begin to cry.

"He loves you! It will hurt him to his soul. If he really loves, you he will respect your honesty and forgive you." Mariah know her uncle very well. He the closest thing she has to a dad.

"What if he doesn't love me?" Jay don't want to hear the answer.

"You're dead!" Mariah wants to see if her own life enough to take the gamble.

"I will tell him." Jay know that she would have to pay for her actions one way or another.

Cash came walking in, pissed that he has take-out food in his hand. This house smells like Thanksgiving Day.

"Baby, damn. I'm sorry. I'm so used to living alone." He leans in for a kiss. Jay greets his lips with hers.

Cash notices her face was covered in tears "What's the matter shawty?" He can't stomach a woman's tears.

"I just ask Jay to be my baby's godmother." Mariah chimes in taking the fast food out of his hand. Begin to eat it, as if she hasn't already eaten.

Jay looks at her in shock. Cash is excited. "Aww that's great! I love the family love up in here." He hugs Jay wiping her face.

"She caught me slipping I got all mushy. I'm honored she asked me." Jay plays along with the song and dance routine.

"We have to go out to dinner tomorrow night to celebrate this unity." Cash cheesing so hard.

"I won't be able to make it Unc. I'll take a rain check you and Jay should still go." Mariah letting Jay know it's her time to come clean.

"Cool! I'm gone hold you to that rain check Miss Greedy." Cash laughs at her.

"I will be looking forward to it."

Mariah exits the room backwards so he

wouldn't see the gun she holding behind

her back.

CHAPTER 31

Zane needs to be alone he has a room all to himself. He glad as hell that he not on the New York trip and close to Shannon. His mind wonders when the phone begin to ring early Friday morning.

He knows it's not Dallas the orders are in place there is no need for them to speak until they return home.

Zane picks up the room phone holding it, "Zane I know you're there," Miesha the front desk clerk says into the handset.

"What do you want ma?" He rude but don't give a fuck at the moment.

"Damn, wow, really?" She with all extra shit. If she had any class about herself, she would have hung up kept it pushing.

"Girl I am not in the mood for any extra shit today! So make it quick." He about to hang up.

"I want to see you." She loves this man. Yet he wouldn't love her back. She can't let go.

"No." He not in the mood. He wants to handle business then go home.

"Why?" she asks, almost in tears.

"It's time I stop playing games with your heart. I will never be the man you want me to be. After this weekend, you will never see me in this state again.

Find someone that will treat you the way you deserve to be treated. It just not me." He keeps it a thousand with her.

She began to cry as she talks. Yet her words fell upon deaf ears because Zane hung up. He knows his actions are wrong. He also knows trying to break it off with her sweetly. Would cause her to beg him to stay as she had before.

Zane still lying in bed his cell phone ring this time Mack's number pops up on the screen. He picks up. "Speak." Zane in dick mode for real.

"What up nigga?" Mack used to his crazy ass pays him no mind.

"Shit, chillaxing" he stated blandly.

"Me, Jasmine, and Dizzy about to go get breakfast, come eat with us." Mack the happiest gangster he ever known.

Zane laughs. "No man, maybe I will catch ya'll at lunch" he assures him.

"Cool family, rest on." Mack about to dead the call when he heard.

"Where's Nisha and Shannon?" Zane thought their mood may have been like his.

"Nisha, that little bitch went out last night. Shannon still sleep she said she would link up for lunch, too." Mack smiles knowing that Zane can't see him.

"Good girl Shannon! Dallas told everybody to lay low. Where is Nisha now?" These damn women are working his nerves with their hard headed asses!

"She ain't back yet." Mack ready to end the call so he could go eat.

"Ok, she should show up soon! It's still early." Zane shakes his head hang up.

He rolls over on his side as he lay in bed naked. Morning wood at its all-time high. Hell, he thinking *"Maybe he should* have given Miesha a lil taste this morning before turning her loose."

Zane golden honey hard body is wrapped in a sheet. He plans to try to get a few more hours of sleep. A knock at the door kills that dream. He hopes its not Miesha. He walks to the door naked snatched it open. Shannon's mouth fell open at the sight and size of his dick. He laughs.

"Girl come in! Quit looking at my dick!" He grabs his basketball shorts that are thrown across a chair in the room.

"I'm sorry, I just didn't expect it to be that big, I mean for you to be naked." She blushing now.

He smiles. "What do you want?" He rude as hell.

She just looks at him like he crazy for a minute. "Nisha left last night she wasn't supposed to. I should have come told you then. So you could've stopped her" she huffs.

"I ain't no damn babysitter. If she wants to leave that's on her. She gotta deal with Dallas about not following orders." He lays the law down.

"You're right about that. What can you do? She's an adult." She has sorrow in her words.

"You okay?" Zane asks thinking his roughness hurt her feelings.

"Yeah" she said while heading for the door.

"No you're not." He steps in front of her.

She looks into his eyes. The tears she has been holding in for the longest came tumbling down. "How could she Zane? How could she?" she cries with her face buried in his bare chest.

He knows the betrayal has done something to her. "I'm sorry Shannon, but I don't know." Her pain is his, he doesn't understand it.

"She just left us for dead. What if Dallas thought our whole crew was a part of this mess she caused?" Shannon is broken behind this nonsense. It kills Zane to watch.

"Baby calm down, okay? I know it hurts. In this life you have to understand that loyalty is hard to find." He hopes she sees his point.

"I know that. I waited damn near all my life to have sex for the first time. At twenty-one when I thought I found him! I

gave it up, got pregnant and dumped all

within six months.

I know this world ain't shit. I just

never thought family would move like

this." She walking around his room now.

CHAPTER 32

Zane notices that she only wearing a night shirt with no panties under it. He shakes his head to take the thought out of his mind. Now isn't the time.

"Baby a nigga done that to you? He a lame, pulling a bad bitch like you gave him confidence. That he never thought he had.

Yes, Jay plays us all, but who are we to stand in the way of love?" This is the first time he has ever asked himself that. Yes, Jay could have handled shit in a different manner. Nonetheless, she has a right to fall in love with whomever she pleases.

"Love? She doesn't know this nigga! How in the hell could she love him?" Shannon is angry now. Hoping Jay hasn't found what she has been looking for her whole life.

"Love can happen when you least expect it. Sure as hell don't want it to." Zane pacing the floor now.

"You love the clerk. After this lick you won't visit this city anymore? Hell, she can come see you." Shannon wants to be encouraging to him. He listened to her cry about her baby daddy and friend.

"I don't love her!" Zane says coolly.

"Oh my fault baby! I thought you had fallen in love yet not ready." She about to leave.

"I did, and I'm not." He says causing her to stop dead in her tracks. Something tells her to keep walking but curiosity got the best of her.

"With who?" Shannon heart jumps into her throat.

"You." Zane lowers his head.

"With who?" Shannon walks close to him to look in his eyes. To see what they say about this ordeal.

"You!" This time he let her look into his soul.

"Oh okay, that's cool!" Shannon turns on her heels walking back to the door.

"That's all the fuck you got to say ma?" Zane steps in front of her for the second time this morning.

"Yeah! What do you want me to say? If you're not ready?" she asks him with her arms folded.

"Make me ready." he steps close to her.

"I can't." She steps back.

"You can!" He steps closer than before.

"Why do you love me?" Shannon wonders aloud.

"I don't know. I have never loved nothing or nobody before." Zane is honest with her.

"What makes me so different?" Shannon asks.

"I'm hoping you're willing to let me find out." Zane face is close to hers now.

The room is getting too small for the both of them. It's like they are gasping for air. "We can see what happens." Shannon mumbles not knowing what she is agreeing too.

Zane lifts her head, she looking into his eyes kissing him. The room begin to spin in circles. Shannon allows her tongue to enter his mouth.

Their tongues danced around inside the two pairs of lips. Zane begin to caress her thighs. She tilted her head back moaning, allowing him to kiss and bite her neck.

Shannon pussy is dripping wet as her juices running down her leg. Zane inserts two fingers inside her. She smirks because she so tight. Shannon hasn't been touched by a man in over a year.

"Damn this shit is tight!" Zane realizes what is happening pulling away from her.

"What?" She still in a daze.

"We shouldn't do this." Zane wants the pussy. She is more than sex to him.

"Zane you said you love me right?" She asks him.

"Yes I do ma, I really do." The words escaping his mouth are blowing him away.

"Well then come get this pussy." Shannon pulls the overnight shirt off fully exposed her body. Zane so hard he forgot all about foreplay. He mounts her, driving his dick deep in those tight walls of hers.

"Aggghhhhhh!" She belts out from pain and pleasure.

"Gotdamn girl!" Zane had all types of pussy before. Nothing close to this right here.

"Fuck me hard nigga" Shannon whispers in his ear.

That shit drives him wild. "Aww that's what the fuck you want?" Zane beating the pussy like he trying to tenderize a piece of meat.

"Oooooh yeah! Zane that's it baby, fuck me!" Shannon loves a man that could throw the dick around.

Zane is feeling himself now. "Shut the fuck up and take the dick." He digs deeper now slow rolling in that juicy fruit.

"Mmmm hummm! Don't tell me to shut up." Shannon on cloud sixty-nine.

"Okay I won't tell you, I will make you." Zane goes ham on her. He flipping her on to her stomach then begin plow driving the pussy.

She yelling, "Oommgg I'm cumming!" Zane doesn't know she is a squirter. Until cum starts spraying all over his chest and stomach. The sight of

that shit caused him to bust in her.

"Oohhh do that nasty shit girl!

Spray it all over daddy." They are shaking

and breathing hard. The knock at the

door throws them off track.

CHAPTER 33

"Who is it?" Zane yells pulling out of Shannon.

"It's me Mack. Hurry up open the damn door!" Zane looks at Shannon as if to say I'm sorry.

She shakes her head saying, "It's cool, open it." Shannon wrapped in a sheet sitting in the bed.

Zane jumps in his shorts snatching the door open. "What man?" He is dripping sweat.

"Man I am looking for Shannon! Have you seen her? Nisha is in the hospital she was beaten up last night."

"What?" Shannon hops out the bed.

"What the hell are you doing over here naked?" Mack shocked.

"Never mind baby! Go get ready meet us in the lobby." Shannon ran out of the room to get dress.

"Aw hell no nigga! You been hitting my baby sister, don't even have the decency to tell a nigga?" Mack put a lot of people in the mind of Chris Tucker when he talks.

"Man fall the fuck back; I will school you later. On how this shit happened. I need to find out what happened to Nisha first," Zane says walking out of the room.

"You damn right we gonna get to the bottom of this shit. Nigga you fucking and carrying on without telling your boy. That's some bullshit!" He looks back at Zane's ruffled sheets he proud of his nigga.

CHAPTER 34

They made it to Providence Hospital Nisha in room 321. She is sitting on the side of the bed with her head wrapped in a bandage. That has a blood stain on the back of it.

Jasmine and Dizzy are already there with her. As soon as they got the call they left IHOP before ordering their food.

Zane walks over to her. "What happened?" He is pissed that she battered and bruised.

"I was at The Platinum Plus talking with this guy named J-Rock. He asks me to walk with him to his car. So I could peep the new rims he put on his ride" She cries.

"Then he asked me to sit in it. I did because I didn't see the harm in it. All of a sudden he started punching me calling me a hard headed slut. Along with other kinds of names." Nisha cries some more. She told the cops her story. Now she has to tell it all over again to Zane.

"He didn't rob you or take any pussy? He just whooped your ass?" Zane is stumped.

"Zane!" Shannon hits him.

"What?" He knows that he is being an ass.

"He just knocked me out then kicked me out the car. I woke up here called Jasmine," Nisha says.

Zane looks at her face its black and blue with bruises. He imagines how black it would look once the healing started. The statement that Nisha made about being hard headed catches his attention.

"Excuse me ya'll, I'll be right back."

As he passes Shannon she asked, "Where you going, boo?"

"To make a call sexy, I won't leave here without you." Shannon smiles as he kissed her exiting the room.

Everyone looks at Shannon and Zane as if they are crazy. Shannon know all eyes are on her so she yells

"What the fuck ya'll looking at me for?" She hates her crew at times.

"Yo ass know why," Mack says causing the whole room to burst out in laughter.

"Shut up bruh," She is glowing.

"You out here acting fast while we trying to get this money. I'm gone whoop yo ass when we get back to the Lou. You know I don't play that shit!" This boy is a complete fool.

Zane could hear the laughter and jokes. He knows they are about him and Shannon. He chuckles as he waits for Dallas to come to the phone.

"Zany Z what it be like my trigger happy potna?" Dallas is a hell of a greeter. The fact that Zane is feeling great didn't hurt.

"Nisha is in the hospital!" he informs him.

"Who? So what ya'll drunk too much last night?" he laughs.

"No, she left the hotel on her own. she got beat up badly." Zane can't stand looking at her.

"Is she in a coma?" Dallas asks nonchalantly.

"No." Zane assures him.

"Is she sitting up and talking?" Dallas asked. Still being quite sly with his tone of voice.

"Yes," Zane says.

"Well send the hard headed bitch home. The condition she's in will only slow you guys down tomorrow." Zane knows Dallas had a hand in the ass whooping Nisha received. He couldn't see some man whooping her ass like that without robbing or raping her.

"Dallas, man why?" Zane hates when Dallas touch a bitch. She could never tell he did it even go to him for comfort.

That's when he would explain that if she had followed the rules she would have been safe. Dallas made them think the rules are to protect them, not control them.

"A hard head makes a soft ass. I bet you that ass is tender right now." He dying laughing after making this statement.

"You're a fucking sicko dude" Zane says before he hanging up.

Zane walk back into the room. Everyone is talking while Nisha asleep. The pain meds finally kicked in.

"How is she doing?" Shannon holding her hand as she sleeps.

"She's doing great actually. They want to keep her overnight for observation. She can leave in the morning" she told him.

"Cool, Dallas wants me to send her home. He says he don't want her hurt any more than she already is." Zane lies.

He hates it, but he can't drop the dime on his boy.

"Aww that's so sweet of him," Jasmine chimes. Mack and Dizzy shake their heads because they know better.

"Yeah that's him heart as pure as gold," Zane lies again.

"Well we're going to stay. You guys can go and get things all situated for tomorrow" Shannon told him.

"You're staying all night?" Zane whines unwillingly.

"Yes she is lover boy," Jasmine teases. She is loving all the love she sees on this man. It reminded her so much of her husband. Jasmine know that he would be on her mind. Until her feet touched down in St. Louis.

"Cool ya'll, let's shake." Zane is pissed. There is something he wants to taste.

"I'll make it up to you daddy." Shannon rubs his chest giving him a light kiss on the lips.

"Oh girl, don't do that daddy shit." Zane has to close his eye for a minute.

"I'm gone whoop yo ass!" Mack fusses at Shannon. "Rub somebody else! Man get your ass out of here." He pushes

Zane out the door. Jasmine and Shannon

watches laughing at them.

CHAPTER 35

The men exit the hospital fast as they enter. The day still young with a lot of planning left to do. The crew on a time limit and itching to act a fool. Zane, Mack, and Dizzy walks into the hotel. The clerk Miesha working second shift today.

She spots Zane and his crew coming through the door. With an attitude, she calls, "Zane, can I speak with you for a minute?"

"What's good ma?" He is short with her.

"I want to know why you trying to play me?" She huffs. As if he owes her something.

"Look boo, I dig what we had but it's over now." He begins to walk away. His crew at the elevator waiting for him.

"I'm pregnant!" she yells out like a typical hood rat bitch.

"So." He keeps walking. As the fellow's eyes almost pops outta their heads.

"What the fuck you mean so?" Miesha barks.

"Bitch, just what I said!" Zane standing face to face with her. She has pissed him all the way off. Mack and Dizzy walks back over to the counter where Zane is. They knew he is about to slap the shit out of her.

"So that's how the fuck you going to play me Zane?" She has the heart of a lion knowing damn well he will beat her ass.

"Look I'm gonna tell you like this. That's not my baby, you and I both know it. Stop bullshitting yourself. If you decide to play this game, I will take the DNA test. When it comes back negative you can kiss my ass." Mack is shaking his head.

The clerk stands there crying because he is right. She is pregnant but the baby doesn't belong to Zane. She has been sleeping with this other guy too. He not trying to hear this baby crap that she talking either. Then decides that she will blame Zane. She looks at him mumbles "I'm sorry."

"You should be." He walks to the elevator never looking back at her.

The trio has everything in motion. The move tomorrow will be so sweet. Zane is wrapping up a call from Shannon. Where she informs him of Nisha's status. He gave her the details on Nisha's flight told her to make sure she on it. She takes down the information then ending the call.

Mack still tripping off Nisha getting beat up. It doesn't seem right. He blurts out, "That shit with Nisha is crazy right?" He shakes his head.

"Dallas set that shit up man." Dizzy know what time it is.

"Get the fuck out of here man. Why would he do some crazy shit like that?" Mack laughs.

"He did it to teach her a hard headed ass lesson." Dizzy schools him.

"No way, he's not that fucked up man." This shit makes Mack mind wonder.

"Yes, he that fucked up! Sometimes these bitches have to learn the hard way," Zane says confirming Dizzy's accusation.

Mack completely blown away by what he learning from talking to his friends. He realizes this game not to be fucked with. You better know what the fuck you're doing. If you plan on being a part of this crew. If you don't Dallas will damn sure teach you.

The night is growing old. The men heads to their rooms to rest up for tomorrow. Shit is in motion Jay and Cash aren't ready for what is in store for them. Zane thinking of the heavy equipment they abstain. It causes him to cringe. He is glad he a part of this team. Not on the other side.

CHAPTER 36

Jay had a sleepless night, thinking about all the shit that has taken place. In a matter of a months. She didn't mean for shit to go this way. Jay never thought she would ever roll over on her own people.

She had to ask herself what kind of woman is she? She knows that her days are numbered. The only thing she can do to make this shit right. Is to come clean as she promised Mariah she would.

Jay stands in the mirror looking at the beautiful woman staring back at her. Who is she? She is dressed to kill in a black sequined Aidan Mattox dress, black

Sedaraby pumps from Neiman Marcus, her neck and wrist are frozen with VVS diamonds.

Jay don't know the woman she looking at. She has stolen someone else's life. Fucked her family in the process because she too selfish to let it go.

Jay walks into the living were Cash is standing. Cash so damn fly wearing a black Giorgio Armani blazer, black and gray button down, gray Armani slacks, and black gators to top it all off.

She touches him on the back, letting him know that she has enter the room.

The Maybach is waiting out front for them. Jay like a princess and a dirty bitch all at the same time. Tonight her fate will be decided. Jay promised herself regardless of what happened she gonna enjoy the moment.

They arrive at the Blue Marlin on Lincoln Street. The place is plush. Jay has only dreamed of eating in a place like this. Being that it's too far out of her reach, but here she is. Jay is living a life that is too good for a person like herself.

Cash sees that something isn't right with her. He doesn't know what. He decided to let it go, assuming that she will feel better once she ate. The waitress catering to their every need.

She is familiar with the way Cash tips. Glad she has him on her ticket tonight. The meal is quite good starting with fried green tomatoes served with a chipotle cream sauce.

The entrée Jay has creamy shrimp and lobster linguine with shitaki mushrooms. Cash has the Chef's selection fresh Mahi Mahi, top with shrimp and crabmeat with garlic mashed potatoes and sautéed green beans. Jay is playing with her food. Cash trying to break the ice with small talk.

"Baby what's wrong? Are you home sick? If you are I will fly, you there whenever you're ready to go." He is willing to do anything to make her happy.

"I'm good love," Jasmine tries to lie. Hell she doesn't have a home to go to. If her feet touch St. Louis, she is dead.

"Well why are you acting like you lost your best friend?" Cash tries to make a joke not knowing she has.

Jay looks across the table at this wonderful man. "Cash I need to come clean" she told him.

Cash sits straight up in his chair. "Come clean then." His heart is hurting already doesn't want heard what she has to say.

"When I came here, I came for the wrong reasons." She is beating around the bush.

"What the hell did you come here for Jay?" Cash hates when people bullshit.

"I came here to rob you." Jays spills the shit as she promised.

"Why?" What did I do to you?" Cash is appalled by that shit.

"Nothing, it's just what my crew and I do to make a living. We teamed up with a group of men that does the same thing. They were laying on you. They couldn't get close to you. That's where I came into play." Jay is glad she got it off her chest.

"So what now?" Cash is bleeding internally behind the news.

"Nothing. I fell in love and fucked my team over for you. I'm sure they will be gunning for me sooner or later. I won't blame you if you kill me. I'm going to get it one way or another." Jay doesn't give a fuck anymore.

"I don't know what to do." Cash says as he calls the waitress to bring the check. The waitress came fast with the check. She knows that a five-hundred-dollar tip is hers. She smiles as they exit the restaurant.

The ride home was like going to a funeral. Cash didn't say shit to her. He stares out the window the whole time. The ride seems a lot longer than it did when they were going to the restaurant. The car pulls up in front of the house.

As the driver door opens, Jay looks at Cash before stepping out asking, "You coming?" The driver closed the door back. He gave the orders to drop her off at the house. Cash going to the airport. When shit get real in his world, he takes the red eye to Vegas to clear his mind. To make the decisions that needs to be made.

She doesn't know how the man moved so strong as he does. Cash has six armed guards waiting in the house. They been ordered to keep her in, and everyone else out. Cash made it crystal clear that his niece Mariah has to go home.

Jay is terrified. She doesn't know when she would see daylight again. She made the bed its time lay in the muthafucka. Jay thinking about hitting the safe and leave.

Cash change the code it works for his or her hand but with these niggas posted outside that plan is dead.

Cash peels away from the house, never noticing the two black corvettes park up the street from his crib because they aren't out of place.

This area made of money. Zane and Mack are in one car and Shannon, Jasmine, and Dizzy occupied the other. They watch the couple's every move tonight. They aren't sure why Jay is left home alone or why the guards have magically appeared. None of that really matters because Dallas's plans don't change for any muthafucka. It's now or

never.

CHAPTER 37

There are two men post outside the driveway leading to the house. They aren't heavily armed from the looks of it. Shannon and Jasmine jump out the Vette acting like two bitches coming from the club.

They staggered towards the two men who were engaged in conversation. One of the men spots Jasmine her thick body hugged by a latex cat suit of course she is wearing red bottoms. It's the only shoes to wear when blood going to be shed.

Niggas will be niggas on guard or not. Pussy is a weakness for ninety-five percent of them.

"Damn ma can I go with you?" He thinks she a bitch with her own money living out here.

"You talking to me daddy?" She turns her sexy up on his dumb ass. He begins walking towards her never noticing that Shannon has the red beam aimed at his head.

She pulls the trigger quickly. He never feels the desert eagle blow his brains out. Jasmine watches his body drop to the ground. She steps over him walking toward the house. The second guard aimed for her but he isn't on point Dizzy domed him from the back.

Now the outside goons are down, there are four more to take out plus Jay. Not before she shows them where the money is.

Shannon walks up the pathway, the man asks "Ma'am can I help you?" Shannon doesn't respond, but Jasmine do.

"No, you need help!" She sprays the place hitting the two idiots that are covering the grounds. Dizzy lives for the kill.

He has the 12-gauge shotgun ready.
Dizzy creeps back to the main entrance
blowing the man's talking on the phone
head clean off his fucking body. The last
man sees the nigga's head explode it
made him throw up.

He tries to run but he catches a
bullet to the knee cap. Dizzy is toying
with him. He loves seeing a bitch nigga
sweat.

The nigga tries to crawl as if he
going some fucking where. Dizzy hit him
again blowing his arm off this time. The
man begs "Fuck nigga just kill me
already." Dizzy loves his heart.

"Aye your gangster! I like that! Too bad it's not gonna save your life today." He turns the nigga's face into mincemeat.

Jasmine place the small door bomb on the door. They step to the side as it blows the lock off.

Dizzy yells at Zane *"Let's move!"* Zane and Mack are already past the corpses that are laid out. They pulled the two at the driveway into the yard toss. Them behind the tall bushes that hiding the yard from the neighbors.

Jay has changed into her sleeping clothes. She has a bowl of ice cream in her hands, she drops it as the door flew open. She is about to take off running when she hears,

"Bitch don't move! I have no love for you! Please don't make me dome you before you show us where the money is." Jasmine's words cut her worse than any bullet ever could.

Jay froze in her tracks staring at the people that she loves with all her heart. "I'm not going anywhere sis." She makes the words fall from her mouth.

"Don't sis me, we're not family!" Jasmine keeps cutting her without a knife.

"Fuck this bullshit ass love connection ya'll got going on. Show us where the fuck the money is so we can lay your ass down, be done with this shit. I know the boys gonna show their ass soon. I ain't going to jail. I'll take hell first." Shannon says.

They have their weapons drawn on her. She knows that her best move is to take them to the money. She walks down the long hall using her hand to open the safe. Zane shakes his head thinking how simple this bitch nigga Cash is to trust a bitch this much, this fast.

Cash got word from the lookout posts a block away. That is circling the house every hour. He gave him them cue to kill everything moving, including Jay.

There is a crew of ten that begin to creep up to the house. Zane and Shannon are bagging money stacks as fast as they could when they heard shots fired.

Zane tells her to keep bagging. He came up the hall sees Jay, Jasmine, and Dizzy laying muthafuckas down as they came through the door. He shocked that she is helping them.

Zane let the tech he holding spit, and it chops down two of the eight niggas left standing. Dizzy is hit but that shit doesn't move him.

He yells out, *"That shit just made my dick hard!"* Dizzy let the P-89 destroy the rest of the. Niggas are falling like they are in Baghdad.

Shit is wicked this shit is worse than Scarface movie Dizzy was Al Pacino.

Mack is hit also Jasmine sprays her way out of the house just in case more are coming. Shannon and Jay both are following her carrying bags of money.

They make it to the car while Zane and Dizzy shut shit down in the crib. They scooped Mack up even though he is yelling, "Leave me it's not enough time to save me!" Blood ran from his mouth as he spoke.

Zane just couldn't leave him. They put him in the car the girl's peels off. They made it to the Super 8 motel where a room is waiting for them.

They know that in an hour their ride will be outside to get them. They couldn't wait to get the hell out of South Carolina. When they pull up they realized the time their ride is already there. It's time to go.

As they make their way into the room they are informed, *"We got to move! This shit has already hit the news. We got about an hour before they shut the highway down looking for the muthafuckas that caused this massacre."* the driver heads out the door. The girls follow him, putting six duffle bags of money into two minivans.

Shannon looking around for the men. When Zane whipped whips into the parking lot. As soon as he jumps out the whip, she ran and hugging him. She sees sadness on his face. "What is it?" She asks.

"Mack's hurt bad." Zane feels fucked up.

Shannon walks over to the car seeing that Mack in the backseat bleeding everywhere. He shot nine times. She wants to save him Make can see it in her eyes. "Sis, don't worry about me." Blood gushes out of his nose.

Shannon shakes her head to blinking back the tears that are threatening to fall. Mack doesn't want to see her cry. "Don't you dare, take care of my brother for me. He never been in love before." She nods her head.

Shannon wants him to stop talking. The more he did the more blood came out of his mouth and nose.

"I will," she promised.

"Goodbye sis, I know the short time we shared I have grown to love you. I'm going to see my family that left me here." Mack gargles on his blood closing his eyes. His breathing ceases.

Shannon wants to die with him. She has never lost anyone close to her. Zane sees that she about to fall he catches her.

The driver yells, *"He's dead! Let's go!"* Zane gives her a push she runs ahead jumping in the van that Dizzy is driving. She doesn't want to ride with Jasmine and Jay. Zane looks back at Mack's lifeless body wipes away the tears. He doesn't want Shannon to see them.

Zane in the second van as it follows the first van out of there. They are heading for the expressway when the crew heard a huge explosion behind them.

Shannon looks back to see what it was. The corvettes blew up in the parking lot of the Super 8. Shannon's heart breaks knowing that Mack was in the back of one of those cars. She beginning to feel like she isn't cut out for this crew.

The ride is smooth sailing. They caused so much havoc in that state. There is no time to search for the culprits. The crew ride in silence. If Mack was with them he would have everyone hyped.

Jay and Jasmine are in the van with a driver named Flex. No one has ever met him but he seems pretty cool. Jasmine plans to quiz Dallas about that cat though. She wonders why Jay is still breathing. All that would come to a head

in due time.

CHAPTER 39

Cash in a fucked up state of mind. He can't go home, broke from what the news says about the home invasion. Cash can't believe these niggas moved like this. He has never seen no shit like this in his life.

This some movie type shit! He right in the middle. No one can link him to the house. He has the deed in some dead white bitch's name. Cash used to fuck with her before she died.

Cash put shit in her name so if he ever got jammed up. He could pin all the shit on her. She was green to what the fuck he was doing. Cash used to hit her off with cake and work.

She was a geek that had the best fucking credit he ever seen. It was easy to put shit in her name houses, business, or cars. He doesn't know what the hell he gonna do now.

Hustling don't come with a fucking retirement plan. All he has to his name is twenty stacks at his apartment in North Carolina. He hasn't seen days like this since he was a child. Now here he is scraping the bottom of the cup all behind a bitch.

Cash has always been told that square love would get him killed. It came with too many emotions. That causes you to let your guard down, and trust the wrong muthafuckas.

He is pissed with himself for being so damn stupid. When the bitch told on herself he should have killed her. Been done with the shit. Now he is laying low at Mariah's crib.

He is glad he paid cash for it or she would have been up shits creek with him. Cash can't have his niece out there like that.

One thing he know though; whoever Jay's crew was he going to find them. They are good as dead. He plans to be on the first thing smoking. Once he gets his money from his apartment in North Carolina.

The crew will pay for his loss one way or the other. His mind doesn't even want to think about Jay. Cash knows that she is with the crew. There is no word of a woman's body found on the scene.

All he could say about her is that she better pray daily. That God takes her before he finds her. He is coming for blood, fuck the money. With hard work and drive he would rebuild the half a million they took from him sooner than later.

Mariah feels like shit seeing her uncle in such a fucked up state. She should have told him what was going on. Before this shit got out of hand. She sees him in deep thought wants to know what his mind was pondering.

"Unc you okay?" She doesn't know what else to ask him.

He looks at her like she crazy. Cash heart aching from the betrayal. The woman he loves has caused, and on top of that he is broke. Mariah understands his pain. "I'm sorry," She said.

Cash feels like shit making her feel bad. When she has done nothing wrong. "No boo, you didn't do anything wrong" he assures her.

Mariah wishes that is true. "Yes I did." She lowers her head.

"What are you talking about Mariah?" He looks at her.

"I know who Jay is" she confessed.

"What the hell you mean you knew?" Cash is pissed he can't believe this shit happening.

"I overheard her in the restaurant bathroom when you first met her. I was telling my baby's daddy I am pregnant. I got sick went into the stall to throw up. Jay came in talking about this dude she is setting up to her friend on the phone. I followed her sees she with you. I feel like shit."

"Why didn't you fucking tell me?" Cash yells at her not giving a fuck at that moment. About the tears falling from her eyes.

"I was planning to tell you when you came to visit me. You were so in love that I don't want to take that away from you.

So I decided to get close to her to see where she was coming from. Once I got to know her she fooled me too. I even told her that I know what she is on.

Jay promises she would tell you because she is really in love with you. I guess that was a lie too." Mariah know she should have killed the bitch. Then called him to handle the rest.

He doesn't know what the fuck to say. Could he really be mad that she didn't want to ruin his happiness? It isn't her fault he got caught with his pants down. Now, his dick in his mouth.

He wants somebody to blame but the truth it's his fault. That bitch is going to pay with her life, and he would die making sure of that.

Cash look at his niece she broken just like him. He couldn't believe how this woman fucked his life up a major way.

"Baby you have no need to apologize. This is my shit I'm gonna fix it." He left before she could respond.

CHAPTER 39

The crew back in the Lou. The
money has been turns in Dallas was
taking inventory so he could pay
everyone. The crew ordered to stay low
key for seventy-two hours. This part of
the reason they have to wait to be paid.

He doesn't want muthafuckas
flossing a few days after a job. Niggas
tend to go over the top when they get
bread. Dallas wants his crew to know
there is more to life than being hood rich.

Dallas wants them to be rich
forever. There's no need to risk your life
still end up living hand to mouth. Most

muthafuckas wouldn't care what you did with your money. Dallas know what it's like to be hungry, homeless, and unhappy.

The world is cold, lonely, and when your money is funny. You see that people really don't give a fuck about you. He wants to be different from any boss that ever lived.

Everybody went on to their respective places. Jay is the only one that has to report to him. He needs to get shit in order real fast because everyone wants to kill her. Dallas ordered that she returns alive he would handle shit from there on out. Dallas has a head strong crew they are pissed with this order. Especially since everyone feels she is the reason Mack lost his life. The crew respects his mind, did as he said, nothing less.

Nisha has been home for a week now. She is almost back to her normal self, physically anyway. She still emotionally fucked up. Dallas know she would be though; he would fix that as well.

She is glad her face is looking better and back to its normal color. Nisha is ready to get the paper that Dallas is holding. At the present time she only has a band to her name. That shit isn't cool at all.

Jasmine back at home with her family. Its feels good to be surround by love. Her husband questioned her about her whereabouts. To see if the lie she'd been telling are going to change.

She laughs in her mind every time he came with the bullshit. Jasmine born to do this shit he just didn't understand that. He even asked about Jay because she basically lives at their house. Some strange reason shit seems to have changed.

He knows his wife. She usually has a fit when Jay doesn't come around but now when he asks she would say, *"Fuck Jay! She's dead to me."* He doesn't understand women at all.

Dizzy back in the hole in the ground he called home. That nigga lives in an underground apartment. Its creepy as hell on the outside. Once you got inside, that muthafucka is laid out.

He has wall to wall plush royal blue carpet that swallows your feet when you stepped on it. The living room has a modern décor all black furniture, smoke glass coffee and end tables, and an eighty-inch flat screen television mounted on the wall.

It's a studio set up. Dizzy has a king sized remote controlled bed that falls from the wall. The nigga using his money right. He hella crazy so he wants his place to be out of sight, out of mind. Not too many people would even chance coming down there to fuck with him.

Shannon has been home with her little baby. She loves that crazy little girl. She thought about Mack and how she didn't have as much time with him as she would have liked. Shannon don't like getting close to people for this reason alone.

The saying, *"It's better to have loved and lost. Than to never have loved at all,"* is pure bullshit. Losing love or a loved one hurt like hell. Only time could heal that wound.

She thinking about Zane too. He has been calling and texting her like crazy. She isn't in the mood to talk to anyone. Shannon grateful to be home with her daughter. That could have easily been her that died in that car. Times like this made her wish she never chosen this life. Even though she knows the life has chosen her.

Now that she down with Dallas there is no turning back. Shannon thought of what he would do to Jay she got chills. Even with all that happened in the past few months of her life. All she really has is her child and Kush.

Zane is lounging around the crib. Bitches has been blowing his phone up like crazy but he doesn't have no rap for none of them. He wishes Shannon would at least let him know she is okay. He knows that she needs space to be with her baby.

Zane never cared about a woman or her child, he does now. Zane just hopes it all worked out. Zane thinks about how Mack left this world with no wife or children. Zane doesn't want to go out like that.

He wants to know at least once in his life what family love feels like. That isn't too much to ask from this sorry ass world. It seems like the hardest thing to get. This time he is going to try no matter what. If not for him, he wants to do it for Mack.

CHAPTER 40

Cash made it to Saint Louis. He has no idea where to start looking for Jay or her crew. He staying at the Hyatt in Union Station. Though he knows his visit going be short lived. Due to money being tight plus the rooms are pricey.

He has to act like a boss to get the info he looking for. Cash chilling in one of the happening clubs in town called Rustic Goat. He is posted in the cut so he could see everyone coming in and out.

This another reason Dallas expressed to his crew to stay low. If you don't kill the person you rob, if they have any heart they coming gunning for you. His crew was ordered to kill everyone in the house when they hit a lick. Cash got lucky.

The club is jumping bad women are everywhere. Even though Cash there on business he sees pleasure that he would love to partake in.

The night growing old he doesn't see anyone that even resembles Jay. Cash found out the Lou was full of thick, plus-sized women that he could fall for after he touch Jay.

Cash heading out the door when he bumps into this bad little chick. She thicker than a down feather comforter.

"My bad shawty," he says.

"Shawty?" She laughs. "Where you from my dude?" She talks like a nigga but it's so sexy to him.

"SC!" he said proudly.

"South Cat?" It's just a lil name that is used in the Lou.

"If that's what you want to call it." Cash plays it cool knowing good and well he has never heard that before.

"What's your name?" She asks him.

"Cash." She looks him up and down. He is fresh, she still laughs.

"What's your name while you laughing at mines?" He talks slick.

"Aja, but my friends call me Venom" she informs him.

"Venom?" He looks at her funny.

"Yeah, I'm poisonous!" She hisses at him.

Cash dick got hard then he says, "Bite me then." She likes his swag.

"One day, not tonight." She hands him a card that has a snake on it. The snake's tongue spells out her name and number.

Cash watches her walk away. He didn't find what he looking for that night;

he enjoyed himself anyhow. He feels

comfort knowing that tomorrow another

day. He heads back to his room feeling a

little better than he did when he arrived.

CHAPTER 41

Shannon's mind has start to get the best of her now. Her daughter's father has picked her up. She needs to get out the house even though she is ordered to lay low.

She thought about hitting the club. She got a funny feeling after remembering what happened to Nisha when she didn't follow the rules. Something about that tells her it's not an accident, but a lesson learned.

She decides to call Zane because the walls in her house are closing in on her, Shannon needs to break free.

Zane steps out the shower his body drips water on his marble floor. The water ran down his chest hitting the eight pack brick abs settling in his navel. He hears his phone ringing when he looks over at it. His heart jumps seeing that Shannon is calling.

"What's good?" Zane plays it cool like it doesn't matter that she'd called.

"I need to see you," she says.

He could hear desperation in her voice. "Baby come on." He gave her his address hanging up.

Shannon hops in her ride heading toward his crib. Never even seeing the

Cadillac CTS following her. As she makes her way to Zane house she listened to Lyfe Jennings *"If I Knew Then What I Know Now."* It's one of her favorite jams. It keeps her calm when she on the verge of losing it.

Shannon pulls into the parking garage of his building. She exits the car looking down at what she wearing, for the first time since she left the house. Shannon wants to kill herself for letting her mind get the best of her.

She has on smoke grey jogging pants, a black wife beater, and Tom from

Tom and Jerry slippers. It's too late now, hell she already there.

The car following keeps straight past the apartment. It was someone to press her if she wasn't following orders. Since she going to Zane's house. The car ordered to keep going and let her be.

Shannon got to his apartment she about to knock on the door. Zane already coming out. "Where are you going?" She looks at him.

"I got to go get my girlfriend." She looks at him he has bumped his fucking head. He told her coming over while he going to pick up some bitch.

"Boy you got me fucked up."
Shannon hit him.

"What?" Zane asks.

"You think you about to pick up your hoe while I'm here?" Shannon barks.

"No the hoe's already here" Zane laughed.

"What?" She smacks him.

He pulls her into the apartment kissing her. She kisses him back then asked. "I'm your girlfriend now?" Shannon wants to hear him say it.

"If you want to be. I got to tell you right now though. I'm not the best nigga in the world because I never had a girlfriend before," he confesses.

"You were a virgin until we fucked a few days ago?" Shannon jokes.

"Hell naw, I just used to fuck hoes - no love. I got trust issues" he told her.

"Why me?" she asks.

"You got trust issues too, that means neither of us want to be hurt. We both want to be loved just never came across the right person to trust." Zane reads her like a book.

CHAPTER 42

"This is true; I don't want you to be my boyfriend." She shocks him.

"Why?" Zane heart feel a sharp pain.

"Every boyfriend I have had lied, cheated, or misused me. I want a man that will hold me, make love to me, share his fears, and life dreams with me." This bitch is deep he thought.

"I can be your man; you can be my woman. That's why I've been single my whole life because all the women I meet *'Bands a make her dance'*." Zane dance around Shannon laughs.

"As we both know I make my own bands. I only dance when my man asks me too." She smiles at him.

"Come here boo." Zane feels weird on this mushy shit, yet it feels right.

Zane cook dinner for them as they talk for what seem like forever. This is the kind of woman older men spoke of. He never believed that any left. Shannon is funny, smart, cute and a certified goon too.

He knows he has to be careful with this one. She might dome his ass if he steps to her wrong. Secretly that shit turned him on.

Shannon went to take a shower because she is getting sleepy. She came out of the bathroom in one of his collared shirts looking sexy as hell.

"You coming?" she asks as if she at home. Zane place the shit compares to hers.

"Yeah ma." He gets up to follow her to the bedroom.

Shannon get under the covers on the side of the bed he usually sleeps on. He doesn't mind this the first time he shared his bed with anyone. Zane has never take a woman to his home. He walks over to the stereo.

"Do you mind? I usually go to sleep to music you know. If it makes feels like someone is here with me." he told her.

"Go ahead I sleep the same way for the same reason" she states.

He turns on his favorite cut *"When We Make Love"* by Ginuwine. He loves this cut. The boy on his grown man shit. He gets in bed nude as always. She still has the shirt on when he tells her,

"You can't sleep in my bed with a shirt on."

"Why?" Shannon smiles.

"You see me? Clothing is not allowed in this bed." Zane serious.

Shannon remove the shirt. "Is that better mister?" she teases.

"Yes ma'am." He holds her in his arms.

Neither of them are sleepy, they just lay there enjoying the song on repeat. She has never feels so close to someone so soon. Shannon mumbles, "I love you." He looks at her kissing her.

"No you don't, you just think you do." Zane is scared of this woman because he loves her too.

"Yes I do." She kisses his chest he closed his eyes because his body was on fire. Ginuwine isn't helping. She kissed down his chest to his pelvic bone. Then licked his V formation. That shit feels so good he moans. Shannon warm mouth makes contact with his penis. The small circles, slurping, and deep throating caused him to lose his mind.

"Damn girl, don't do that shit like that." She keeps going taking all of him into the back of her throat. Zane was shocked because he twelve inches all the way.

Shannon continues to make it disappear with ease, and he wants to taste this lady too. It's unfair for her to treat him this good. *"Ahhh ooohhh."* Zane moans. "Let me taste you boo," he begs in a low tone.

"No, tonight is my night. Let me do me" Shannon demands, driving him insane. She mounts him letting him feel her wetness sliding down his pole. As if she a stripper. She moans as he enters her soul. *"Mmm suuu hummm,"* she hisses.

Zane palms her ass as she rides his pipe like she an equestrian. He loving every damn minute of it. *"Ohhhh shit baby."* He never made this much noise ever. Shannon making his toes curl. She rocks back and forth enjoying herself.

While getting caught up in the music, moving to the beat. Shannon arches her back Zane has to close his eyes to keep the tears from falling that's forming in his eyes. Zane even holds his breath from time to time.

Shannon in a world of her own now. Softly she moans *"Zane, oh Zane, give it to me daddy!"* He enjoying this rollercoaster his woman taking him on. For the first time in his life he making love with someone he loved. She on the verge of cumming.

She begins to rock faster forcing him deeper inside her walls. Shannon whispers, *"Cumming ooohhh Zannnne, I'm cumming."* He lost it at that moment came with her. Shannon lays flat on top of him. He is still inside of her yet she fast asleep.

Zane wraps his arms around her kissing her forehead. Zane lays there listening to the music enjoying the space he in. He opens his eyes allowing the tears he has been holding in his whole life to fall whispering, *"I love you, too."*

Shannon heard him because she isn't fully asleep. It made her press her body closer to him embracing what lies ahead of them.

CHAPTER 43

The sun shining through Zane's bedroom window. Shannon is still on top of him the phone begins to ring. Zane hopes it isn't any thirsty bitch because that is dead from this point on.

He grabbed the phone off the marble topped nightstand. Zane sees Dallas calling he picks up. "Hey family." His voice has music in it. He grabs his stereo remote to kill the music that still playing.

"Well great morning my nigga," Dallas smiles on the other end of the phone.

"Yeah, it is a great morning boss." Zane looks down at his sleeping beauty.

"I need for everyone to meet me at the warehouse at five p.m. today. It's payday." Dallas always says that when it's time to pass out money.

"I'm on it family, everyone will be there for sure," Zane assured him.

"Make sure Dizzy's crazy ass shows up. I don't have time to chase that nigga to give him his money." Dallas doesn't understand Dizzy. He just fucks with him because Zane vouched for his ass.

"I will make it my business to get him there" Zane laughs.

"Okay then my nigga." Dallas was about to let him go.

"Until then," Zane says.

"Oh yeah! Tell Shannon I said great morning." Dallas burst out laughing.

"Will do, will do." Zane hangs up on Dallas's laughter. It gets under his skin sometimes the way Dallas keeps tabs on people's whereabouts. He knows that he would have to school Shannon on following orders. If she doesn't Dallas would have someone press her the same way, he did Nisha. If that ever happens Dallas a dead man.

Shannon begin to wake up tries to pull her body off of his. He grabs her kissing her. This loving side of him is wild to her.

"Thanks daddy. I got to move around get myself together." Shannon walks to bathroom for a hoe bath. So she could drive home to get a real bath and change clothes.

"That's cool love we got to meet with Dallas at five. It's payday." Zane don't give a damn for real. He good on paper.

"I'll be there!" She throws her clothes on walking out the door. Zane watches her leave and pull off his street.

Shannon feeling really good hoping what she feeling is real.

She knows with any relationship only time will tell. She going to flow with it play it by ear. That's one of the hardest things for a woman to do. Sometimes that's just the way shit is.

Shannon made it home in about twenty minutes, taking her bath, and figures she needs a nap. First she has to let the girls know about payday. She knows this will be music to Nisha's ears. She hasn't heard from her since she had been sent home.

Jasmine picks up the phone with her signature "What do you want bitch?" It's their way of showing sisterly love.

"Call Nisha on three-way," Shannon says she is sleepy as hell.

Jasmine conference Nisha on the call. "Hey." She sounds as if she still sleeping and high.

"This bitch Shannon is on the phone too," Jasmine told her.

"What's the word?" Nisha asks.

"Dallas wants us to be at the warehouse at five p.m.," she states.

"I hope he got that money." Nisha is awake now.

"Yeah, Zane told me its payday"
Shannon confirms.

"That's what I wanted to hear."
Nisha is happy now.

"Bitch why he always calling you to
telling us shit?" Jasmine asks.

"Zane didn't call me! I was at his
house when I woke up to leave he told
me" Shannon bursts Jasmine's bubble.

"Woke up!" Nisha yells.

"Leaving?" Jasmine says.

"Yeah!" Shannon says.

"Hell no bitch! You gonna tell us
what happened. Why you're sleeping at
Zane's house," Jasmine said.

"Right" Nisha cosigns.

"I will school you hoes later. I need all ya'll to know that he my man now." Shannon hangs up on their nosy asses.

Jasmine makes a memo to kick her ass later. She ends her call with Nisha plan to get her day moving. She preparing herself for the argument. Jasmine will have with her husband in order to leave the house.

This movement new to her husband. He getting tired of it believes she is cheating. Jasmine keeps telling him that she isn't, but he not buying that shit. Jasmine has to do what she had to

do when duty calls.

CHAPTER 44

Cash linked up with Aja for lunch. He wants to pick her brain to see if she knows about the streets' movement around her city. They went to Houlihan's located in the lower level of the mall.

Aja came dress like she going to the club in black skinny jeans, red half shirt with double C's on it, oversized shades and a Chanel bag. She fresh to death, Cash thinks she fucking with a major player.

Aja greets him with a hug. She feels good in his arms even though she isn't as thick as Jay. He pulls her seat out for her. This new to her the men around here don't move like that.

"I see you date them go getters by your attire" he jokes with her.

She laughs, "I am the go getter." Aja puts him on game without telling her business.

"Oh really? So you know who to go to if a nigga need to move them thangs?" Cash begins picking her brain.

"I might." She sly about the shit. "Why? You need a connect here? I thought ya'll was getting it down there?" Aja picking his brain now.

Cash half lies. "I'm the man in my city. Some niggas down my way got to hating. Touched my cheese while I was out of town on business." She looks at him as if a narc.

"Really!" Aja not impressed with his story. Mainly because you couldn't pay a muthafucka fuck with her crew.

"I don't know you well enough to lie!" Cash lies again.

Aja can't read him so she refuses to talk business with him. She will run his street name by Vicious. See what she knows about dude. Aja changed the subject enjoyed her lunch. She likes dude he pretty cool.

Hell, she thought Sean was cool too. Boy was she wrong about him. She decided that she isn't taking any chances with Cash. Aja walking a very fine line. She has too much to lose, her sister's trust would be the first thing to leave if she fucks up.

They parted ways Cash feel a little closer to his target. Thinking whoever she down with might just be the people he looking for.

Zane manages to get Dizzy's crazy ass out of his house. He even went to pick the nigga up. When he owns a damn Benz. This dude weird as hell but he family. Dallas wants him there. Its Zane's job to make it happen. Something has to be going on because Dallas usually don't press Dizzy much. So for him to ask for his presence its major.

"I don't know why I gotta come," Dizzy gets in the car bitching. He needs to get his ass out that house living like a hermit crab.

"Man just come the fuck on." Zane not about to let this nigga get on his nerves today. Not after the night he had.

"Aye man don't be talking reckless to me." Dizzy extra today.

"Nigga," Zane says he shut the fuck up. He crazy, but not insane enough to fuck with Zane. He rides with headphones on like the music in the car is off. Zane looks at him shaking his head.

He wondering if this nigga mama drank or did drugs while carrying him. Maybe she dropped his ass when he came out. Its four fifteen so they heading to the place to be.

The women are in route as well. They all rode in Nisha's new whip seeing no point in having all their cars going to the same damn place. They talked a little shit. Shannon told them about her night with Zane. How they got to the point of fucking in the first place.

Nisha feels like she missed out on all the good shit. She still a little emotionally torn but she tries hard not to let it be known. She not fooling anyone though. If somebody moves too quickly, she jumps. Nisha get back to her old self sooner or later. It's her own fault she stepped out in the line of fire. In a city she doesn't know shit about that's a fool's move. The ride is smooth they pulled up about five minutes after Zane and Dizzy.

The women jump out the car. Nisha asks "Where is Mack crazy ass?" No one told her Mack dead.

Everyone looks at her as if crazy. Shannon says, "He's dead." Nisha wasn't ready for the words that left her friends mouth. She walks away from the crowd heading toward the building. Zane feels bad for her. He knows that Dallas has plays with her mind.

CHAPTER 45

Dallas opens the door greeting everyone with a hug. When he got to Nisha he holds on to her. "I am so glad your better boo. That shit had me spooked to think one of my girls got hurt." Zane almost laughed. Shannon could smell bullshit coming from his mouth.

"Yeah, I'm better." Nisha holds him tight.

"You see why I make rules? I don't want this world to hurt you." Dallas looks in her eyes.

She hangs on to his every word. The man is good at what he did. "Your right daddy." Those words let him know she is sold to the highest bidder him. From there on out she would forever do what he told her. Exactly how he told her to do it.

The whole room watching this stage play that Dallas is putting on. Nisha feels like she is protected in his arms. There isn't shit anyone in the world could tell her from there on out. Dallas is her hero. Nisha needs someone to comfort her no one ever has until now.

The man releases her to sit at his desk making her feel like a queen for the moment. Then Dallas got right down to business. "I want to thank everyone you for the hard work you all put down for your family.

The news is still talking about the damage ya'll caused. The pigs so deep down there right now. They making it hard for them niggas to eat." He is proud of his crew.

"A half a million is bought home. Everyone here will get fifty thousand before you leave. Twenty-five thousand will be deposit in the trust fund. I am building for each of our retirements.

What we do is not meant to be a long

term job. I suggest you trouble your brain

for something you would like to invest in.

Within the next year cause this shit is

short lived."

The women are with that because

they don't want to live the rest of their

lives this way.

Zane and Dizzy are used to it. They

already have money in their trust. Dallas

a business man in every way. He will

forever make sure his family straight. Not

just for today but forever.

Dizzy is here so he has to show his ass. "So what happens to this Jay bitch that fucked the crew? Also caused Mack to lose his life?" The feeling in the room became dark.

"That's why I called you all here. I'm glad you made it Dizzy" Dallas states.

"I don't want to be here so it better be good. I could have gotten my money at some other time." He lets his feelings be known.

"I'm glad to see you too, Dizzy." Dallas fucks with him.

Dizzy waves like man go on with that bullshit. Dallas laughs. "Well let me make my point so Dizzy can get back to his busy life." The room fills with laughter because everyone know that nigga isn't going to do shit but go home play his game.

"I want the crew to stand and give Jay a round of applause." She came from the back looking flawless. No one clapped. The room lost with what is going on here.

"I guess you all mad at her right?" Dallas asks.

"Hell yeah." They all began to fuss about how she should be dead already.

"Cool it ya'll." They are still fussing.

That's when Dallas barks, "Shut the fuck up!" The room stops moving the heat is still heavy in the air. They have to hear him out because shit is crazy right now.

"Jay did not rollover on her family. Everything she did, I orchestrated it." The room is really lost now. "I needed her to play this part without anyone getting in her way. Jay has been down with me before the rest of the women starts.

Nisha, how do you think I know to kidnap you to get money out of West?" Nisha looked looks dumbfounded. "I just thought you were watching me," She states.

"No, Jay lead me to you baby."

Dallas know this is a lot to swallow.

"So she never loved Cash for real?" Jasmine asks hoping she isn't because she missed her friend terribly.

"Hell no! I was doing my job. I'm sorry it had to be this way. It was a sure fire plan; I won't take the blame for Mack's death. That's my dude Shannon what have you always ask when we pull a smooth move?" Jay speaking for herself this time.

"Are you ready to die?" Shannon says. Everyone in the room knows in this line of business you can lose your life.

The crew can't believe that Dallas's slick ass fooled them. This nigga is the master of the minds.

"See, she risks her life for all of us. The nigga's niece even overheard her talking on the phone to you, Shannon. She could have been dead after that. The nigga was so in love. That his own niece couldn't bear to break his heart by diming Jay out" he informs them.

"That's the little girl we saw you with?" Shannon states.

"Yes, she befriends me to see where my heart and head is. I gamed her young

dumb ass too." Jay proud of her work.
She just wished Cash was dead.

"Damn you're a cold-blooded ass
bitch." Jasmine gives her a hug. "I missed
you." Shannon and Nisha runs over
hugging her too.

Dizzy and Zane laughs. "You a grimy
ass nigga Dallas." Dizzy has to say that
shit. Since he knows everyone is thinking
it.

The world is good again. Their girl is
back in the family fold and counting the
money right. Nisha is feeling brand new
again with a different outlook on life. How

she plans to spend her money. Zane walked over to Shannon kissing her.

"Hold up my man! What you doing kissing one of my girl?" Dallas teases knowing damn well they are a couple now.

CHAPTER 46

Zane points to Jay, Jasmine, and Nisha. "Those are your girl's right there, this my woman." He holds Shannon tight and they all laughed.

"I know that shits right! I'm happy for you bruh. I wanted you to the have her the day you fell in love with her." Dallas let that slips on purpose.

"When did you fall in love with me?" Shannon looks up at him.

"The first day you walk through these doors," Zane admits.

"Aww" The crew chimes.

"I just love black love," Dizzy says. Everyone shakes their heads because he too damn silly.

"Now that we have things squared away. I want everyone to know in three weeks we hit New York. Nothing hard this time. It will be like taking the sweetness out of a sugar cane." Dallas lays down the law.

Two waiters came in the room. Dallas last statement was their cue to enter the warehouse from the main house. One came in carrying a tray with six envelops on it. He served each member their pay. The other carries glasses of champagne for each member. After the bubbly is served Dallas raised his glass.

"Thanks to the Duffle Bag Bitches, our family is complete. In three weeks we cause damage in the Big Apple. Last but never least, nor ever forgotten. Salute to Mack our fallen warrior. We miss you my nigga." They let their glasses tilt to let some slip for the homie.

"Let's toast to New York and a man gone too soon." They touched glasses yelling, *"To Mack."*

Things are in full swing. The music jumping, the girls talking shit, and teasing each other. Even Dizzy in chill mode playing the game in the warehouse. Shannon sitting on Zane's lap, Dallas on a business call. As Jay and Jasmine talk like they had lost each other for years.

Things looking good from where Zane sat. They have some cool music playing. Zane needs to hear that new Yo Gotti.

"Get up boo," Zane told Shannon.

"Where you going? You leaving?" Shannon asks.

"Not without you! Going to my car to grab a CD" he told her.

She moves out of his way so he could go to the door. Dallas ends his call. "See, she already got you in a thong. You gotta explain your movement and shit." He loves to talk shit with his people.

"Don't worry about mine nigga, I got this." Zane pops his collar.

"Tell him daddy." Shannon strokes his ego.

"See, you hear that?" Zane points to her.

"Man take yo ass to your car. Talk that shit when you come back in," Dallas laughs.

Zane laughing as he steps out the door. He half way to his car when a 45 touched his temple. A voice he doesn't know says to him, "Nigga don't move or you're dead!"

AUTHORS NOTE

HELLO ALL I AM ALICIA C. HOWARD, I WANT TO TAKE THE TIME TO THANK THOSE WHO HAVE SUPPORTED AND SHOWED ME LOVE. I HAVE TO SAY THAT IF YOU WOULD HAVE KNOWN ME A FEW YEARS AGO.

YOU WOULD HAVE SAID SHE WILL NEVER BE A WRITER. THAT'S THE THING I LOVE ABOUT GOD! HE SEES THINGS THAT WE AS PEOPLE TURN THE BLIND EYE TO BECAUSE WE ASSUME THAT ALL HOPE IS LOST.

I HAVE HAD PEOPLE GIVE UP ON ME, USE ME (TRY TO ANYWAY), AND REFUSE TO LOVE ME NO MATTER HOW MUCH OF MYSELF I GAVE. IT MEANT NOTHING TO THEM. I CONTINUED TO BE ME AND GAVE FROM MY HEART.

GOD SAW FIT TO TURN THINGS AROUND FOR ME. WHEN THE WORLD COUNTED ME OUT - HE HELD MY HAND. WHEN THE STREETS TRIED TO SWALLOW ME WHOLE - MERCY SAID NO.

AND HERE I AM TODAY STRIVING TO BE THE BEST ME I COULD EVER BE. NO ONE IS PERFECT BUT I WANT

TO TRY TO GET AS CLOSE AS I CAN.

WHEN YOU LOOK AT ME DON'T LOOK

AT ME AS AUTHOR, FAMOUS, OR

CELEBERITY Because I AM NONE OF

THE ABOVE.

I AM A WOMAN THAT WANTS TO

BE LOVED, I HAVE DREAMS OF BEING

MORE THAN WHAT THE EYES COULD

SEE. I STRUGGLE TO MAKE IT HERE

TODAY FIGHTING FOR AIR, LOVE, AND

LIFE. I HEARD ALL THE THINGS THAT

ARE SUPPOSED TO BE FREE THEY

JUST DON'T COME EASILY. WHAT

I AM TRYING TO SAY IS FOLLOW YOUR

DREAMS NO MATTER HOW FAR AWAY

THEY MAY SEEM. BREATHE FREELY, LOVE AS MUCH AS YOU CAN, MOST OF ALL LIVE LIFE TO THE FULLEST. THANK EVERY ONE OF YOU THAT LOVED AND SUPPORTED ME.

458
2451

878
0747
798
6239

CPSIA information can be obtained
at www.ICGtesting.com
Printed in the USA
LVOW08s1818041116
511689LV00009B/845/P